J Ellis

**The seed basket**

For ministers, Sunday-school teachers, Christian endeavourers

J Ellis

**The seed basket**
*For ministers, Sunday-school teachers, Christian endeavourers*

ISBN/EAN: 9783741181696

Manufactured in Europe, USA, Canada, Australia, Japa

Cover: Foto ©Andreas Hilbeck / pixelio.de

Manufactured and distributed by brebook publishing software
(www.brebook.com)

J Ellis

**The seed basket**

THE SEED BASKET . . .
FOR MINISTERS . . . .
SUNDAY SCHOOL TEACHERS
CHRISTIAN ENDEAVOURERS .
TEMPERANCE AND . . .
CHRISTIAN WORKERS. . .

BEING A COLLECTION OF .
300 SERMON OUTLINES . .
SEED CORN. . . . .
SUNDAY-SCHOOL ADDRESSES
BIBLE READINGS . . .
BAND OF HOPE TALKS . .
ETC ETC . . . . .

COMPILED BY THE EDITOR OF "THE TOOL BASKET "
"FINE WHEAT FROM MANY FIELDS " ETC.

Second Edition

1897
LONDON . . . . .
H. R. ALLENSON . . .
30 PATERNOSTER ROW E.C

BUTLER & TANNER,
THE SELWOOD PRINTING WORKS,
FROME, AND LONDON.

# PREFACE

---

THE very generous reception accorded to " The Tool
Basket," together with many testimonies received as
to its usefulness, has led the editor to send forth this
companion volume, with the desire that it may prove
equally suggestive and helpful.

J. ELLIS.

## TEN QUALIFICATIONS OF A PREACHER

He should be able to preach plainly and in order. He should have a good head, good power of speech, good voice, and a good memory. He should be sure of what he means to say, and be ready to stake body and life, goods and glory on its truth. He should know when to stop. He should study diligently, and suffer himself to be vexed and criticised by every one.

M. LUTHER.

# BIBLE STUDY

## Old Testament and the New

The Old Testament *enfolds* the New Testament, while the New *unfolds* the Old.

The New Testament is *concealed* in the Old, the Old is *revealed* in the New. The *Scriptures* are the Old Testament, the New is the Holy Spirit's commentary on the Old.

Old Testament presents objects to the eye, New Testament words for the ear and heart. No ordinance of the Old Testament is a type of a New Testament ordinance.

Every Old Testament ordinance is a type of New Testament truth.

The Old Testament is a porch or entrance way, a bringing in of the New. Heb. vii. 10.

# CONTENTS.

# THE SEED BASKET

### Absalom's Downfall

*" The way of the ungodly shall perish."*—Ps. i. 6.

Five steps in Downfall.

| | |
|---|---|
| War. | Disobedience. |
| Alone. | Deceit. |
| Guilt punished. | Danger. |
| Expedition failing. | Dishonour. |
| Sorrow of David. | Death. |

### Affliction, Compared

*Paul's scales to weigh our afflictions.*—2 Cor. iv. 17.

| *In one scale.* | *In the other.* |
|---|---|
| Affliction. | Glory. |
| Light afflictions. | Weight of glory. |
| Light affliction for a moment. | Eternal weight of glory. |
| Nothing more. | Far more exceeding. |

### Affliction, Uses of

Isa. xxxviii. 16.

Implies and expresses a truth we are slow to realize.

Severe sickness is not always an unmitigated evil. Life is often lengthened and health invigorated. Afflictions do not come unsent.

Often prove to be messengers of mercy as well as of judgment.

Affliction teaches us our entire dependence upon God.

Affliction disrobes us of self-righteousness.

Affliction brings us to realize and enjoy the fulness of Christ.

Sanctified affliction stimulates us in Christian work.

### Armour, Seven Pieces of

Eph. vi. 14-18.

Girdle of truth (2 Cor. xiii. 8).

Breastplate of Righteousness (Phil. iii. 9).

Sandals of the Gospel (Eph. ii. 10).

Shield of faith (1 John v. 4).

Helmet of salvation (Ps. xxvii. 1).

Sword of the Spirit (Heb. iv. 12).

Prayer keeps armour bright.

### Bible, Alls of the

"All things" occur 221 times. Remember that "all" *means* "all," and not *some*. Here are some :

All things work together, etc. (Rom. viii. 28).

All things are possible, etc. (Mark ix. 23).

All things whatsoever ye ask, etc. (Matt. xxi. 22).

I can do all things, etc. (Phil. iv. 13).

Giving thanks for all things, etc. (Eph. v. 20).

Thirteen "alls" which are very helpful to meditate upon in Psalm cxlv.

Casting all your care, etc. (1 Pet. v. 7).

The Lord shall preserve thee from all evil (Ps. cxxi. 7).

My God shall supply all your need, etc. (Phil. iv. 19).

Christ is all and in all (Col. iii. 11).

### Brazen Serpent

John iii. 14.

Serpent. A sign of crucified Christ.

It reminded of sin. Cross displays the heinousness of sin.

It taught that sin is a vanquished and a powerless oe.

Sin cannot ruin God's servants.

It can only vex and harm them.

It exhibited the plague itself as the means of its own defeat.

Breadth and comprehensiveness of the statement *the world*.

Introduction of new principle—Eternal Life.

### Brazen Serpent

Numbers xxi. 4–9.   John iii. 14.

Discouragement is always from the devil (*v.* 4).

The path of murmuring is full of stings (*v.* 5).

We "speak against God" when we complain o our lot (*v.* 5).

Each new sin brings a new penalty (*v.* 6).

We are reminded of our sin through our suffering (*v.* 7).

Heartfelt confession is a sign of wholesome recovery (*v.* 7).

Looking is believing (*v.* 8).

Look and live—look or die (*v.* 8).

Look not upon faith or feeling but look at Christ (*v.* 9).

### Cain, Sin of

Gen. iv. 13.

1. Shows that the sinner thinks more of his punishment than of his sin.

2. That he sets up to judge God.

3. That he is as much a rebel by despair as once he was by rebellion.

4. That he still refuses to bring the right sacrifice.

### Cedar Tree, Lessons from Psalm xcii. 12

POINTS FOR CHRISTIANS.

*Excellent* figure as to growth symmetrical consistency in life.

*Majesty.* Branches spread.   Christians should shelter and protect.

*Found* in all countries.   So grace should and does help all men everywhere to live Christian lives.   Instance, Fiji, Africa, Greenland, and China.

*Strongest* of trees.   Abiding, old age.

*Fragrant.* Scent of Lebanon reaches a long way. So Christians by their life diffuse their influences. Felt presences useful.

*Useful.* Largely used for pencils, etc.   So Christians should be useful in all ways and purposes.

### Characteristics of the Christian Age

John xvi. 23–27.

I. *Complete Revelation.* (1) The subject: the Father, His nature; God; His character, love; His purpose, Salvation.

(2) The medium, Christ, the Son, Mediator, Ambassador, Revealer.

II. *Adequate Illumination.* (1) Clear, no longer in parables, proverbs, or veiled forms, but easy propositions (*v.* 25). (2) Sufficient, no need other than Spirit's teaching.

III. Perfect communion. (1) In the part of Christian liberty in prayer. Ask anything (*vv.* 23-26). Success in prayer guaranteed by using Christ's name. Saviour's intercession (*v.* 26). Father's love (*v.* 27) on the part of the Father. (2) Loving Christ's people (*v.* 27). Granting their requests (*v.* 23).

IV. Augmenting exultation. (1) The nature of it. Joy of Christian is inward, spiritual, progressive, and permanent.

Lesson 1. Superiority of the Christian age over others. 2. The increased responsibility of all who live in it.

### Christ Crucified
#### Luke xxiii. 33-46.

Crucified Saviour (*vv.* 33-35).
Cruel soldiers (*vv.* 36-38).
Converted sinner (*vv.* 39-43).
Clouded sun (*vv.* 44, 45).
Committed Spirit (*v.* 46).
Cross is our shame or our glory (*v.* 34).
True repentance never too late (*v.* 41).
Cross of Christ is the key of paradise (*v.* 43).
By the Cross to Crown, no other way (*v.* 46).

### Christ, Mind of
#### Phil. ii. 5.

The aim and ideal of the Christian to be like Christ.

Illustrate some of the chief features in the character of Jesus by incidents in His life.

Humility :—Washing feet of disciples.
Courage :—Denouncing Pharisees.
Compassion :—Healing Bartimæus.
Forgiving Spirit :—Peter.
Fondness for children :—Taking them in His arms.
Love for all men :—Crucifixion.
Prayerfulness :—Nights on the mountain.

## Christ, Mind of

Phil. ii. 5.

His patient mind (Luke xxii. 25).
His gentle mind (Luke xxii. 26).
His humble mind (Luke xxii. 27).
I seek *not* Mine own will (John v. 30).
I do *nothing* of Myself (John viii. 28).
I have *not* come of Myself (John viii. 42).
I seek *not* Mine own glory (John viii. 50).
He came "to minister" (Mark x. 45).
His gracious mind (Luke xxii. 28).
His faithful mind (Luke xxii. 29).
His prayerful mind (Luke xxii. 32).
His trustful mind (Luke xxii. 32).
His obedient mind (Luke xxii. 37).

## Christ on the Cross

Mark xv. 22-37.

Sin cannot be conquered by anodynes (*v.* 23).
No human device can give victory over Satan
(*v.* 23).
The crucifixion demonstrates the love of God and
the cruelty of man (*v.* 25).
Sin stops at nothing (*v.* 25).
See what sin deserves (*v.* 25).
　Shame for its audacity.
　Scorn for its pretension.
　Ridicule for its folly.
　Punishment for its guilt.
The cross is our shame or our glory (*v.* 27).
Only hearts' blood can save hearts (*v.* 30).
Men mock the Master when they mock His ser-
vants (*v.* 31).
We want to "see and believe" when we substitute
eye for heart, experiment for faith, intellect for spirit-
uality (*v.* 32).
He took the "place" of the "forsaken" that we
might take the place of the accepted (*vv.* 22-34).
(Eph. i. 6).
What belief derides, faith rejoices to accept (*v.* 32).

## Christ, Precious Blood of, and its Sevenfold Blessings

1 Pet. i. 18, 19.

By it we have Redemption (Eph. i. 7).
By it we have Justification (Rom. v. 9).
By it we are cleansed from sin (1 John i. 7).

By it we are sanctified (Heb. ix. 13, 14).
By it is our peace made with God (Col. i. 20).
By it we are brought nigh to God (Eph. xi. 13).
By it we shall overcome (Rev. xii. 11).

### Christ our Example

1 Pet. ii. 21.

*As God's Son.*   Submission (John vi. 38).
Dependence (John v. 30).
Confidence (John xi. 41, 42).
*To Men.*   Obedience to parents (Luke ii. 51).
Kindness to others (Matt. ix. 36).
Lowliness (Luke xxii. 27).
Gentleness (1 Pet. ii. 21-23).
Forgiveness (Col. iii. 13).
*His Mind.*   Humility (Phil. ii. 5).
Self-denial (Matt. xvi. 24).
Holiness (Heb. vii. 26).
Love (Eph. v. 2).

### Christ the Bread of Life

John vi. 25-35.

Eat to live, but do not live to eat (*v.* 27).
Spiritual interests should be supreme (*v.* 27).
The seal of God is the power of the Holy Spirit.
We are saved by God's mercy, not by our merit ;
by Christ's dying, not by our doing (*v.* 29).
The foundation of everything is taking Christ at
His Word (*v.* 29).   2 Pet. i. 5-7.
It is the glory of God to give (*v.* 32).
Jesus Himself is the answer to every cry of the soul
(*v.* 35).
. The worldling is satiated, only the believer is satis-
fied (*v.* 35).

### Christ the Life and Light of Men

John i. 4.

Christ's life so radiant that it fills our life with light.
God life without pause or interruption.
Christ the true life.   A life of highest knowledge,
of the moral nature of God, the spiritual nature of
man, and the true relations between God and man ;
three-fold in its contents, and the blended result of
perceptions of heart, intellect, and conscience.
A life of perfect love.   Love is the grandest form

of life, because it includes all other virtues which without it are nothing.

In the light of men because it is a glorious revelation, a great quickening power.

If we place ourselves in the light of Christ's life, we realize a change in our thoughts, heart, conscience, and will.

### Christ the Rock of Salvation

Ps. lxi. 2.

Show me the way. Reveal Jesus.
Enable me to tread it. Work faith in me.
The heart's cry and desire.

1. A recognition of a place of safety.
2. A place abundantly sufficient when our personal weakness has been realized.
3. The place must be attained by Divine help and hand.
4. Character of the refuge and position.

Refuge a rock, and position of a believer upon a rock.

Infinitely higher is the salvation of God than we are.

### Christ worth Seeing

Luke iv. 20.

Fastened—fascinated.

1. Christ arrests attention by His claim : God Man, Son of God. By His sinlessness; separate and singular—surely the sinless one is the authoritative one. By His sacrifice; cross is a problem for human thought. By His resurrection : veritable and questionless historic fact.
2. I need a Christ who is incarnate God that I may know God.

I need a Sinless Christ for my example.

I need a vicariously sacrificing Christ for my forgiveness.

I need a Risen Christ to meet my death fearlessly.

3. It will give us hope, rest, and control our conduct.

### Christ's Absence and its Expediency

John xvi. 7.

All departures are painful : Boy to school ; girl to marriage ; friend to sea ; death.

Christ was more to disciples than they realized.

I. It would prove to be a present spiritual power.

Twofold assurance. He would be always with them, and His spirit also.

Child Christian wants a Christ in the flesh. He was outside us. He is in us now.

II. It localises our conception of heaven. Gone to prepare a place.

III. It gives ground for cherishing a high hope. Becomes a spiritual power, holy example, call, and impulse. Hope of reunion. Go no more out for ever.

### Christ, Eleven Appearances of

Were not only proofs of His resurrection, but pledges of His love. Not indiscriminate comings and goings, but definite appearances to teach us special lessons.

1. To Mary weeping by the tomb, Mark xvi. 9. Jesus always present in our sorrow.

2. Women returning from the tomb, Matthew xxviii. 9. No act of living service but is rewarded by His presence.

3. Peter, Luke xxiv. 34. Held in specific memory. His love is changeless, not dependent upon our constancy or moved by our stumbling.

4. Two going to Emmaus, Luke xxiv. 31. As we walk, if we talk with Christ, shall realize His presence.

5. Apostles at Jerusalem, Thomas absent. John xx. 19. Lose much if we absent ourselves from assemblies of the saints.

6. All the disciples at Jerusalem, John xx. 26. The patience of Jesus, in the presence of doubts in stooping to our unreasonableness, should break our hearts in love.

7. Seven disciples fishing, John xxi. 1–11. Look away from self and failure. His resources never fail. Stop trying and trust.

8. Eleven disciples on the mountain, Matt. xxviii. 16. Meet Him upon the Mount, and then go down to bless others.

9. 500 brethren at once, 1 Cor. xv. 6. Jesus with the multitude to bless.

10. James, 1 Cor. xv. 7. The first disciple that was martyred. Christ will prepare us for every trouble.

11. Eleven disciples at His ascension, Acts i. 11. The thought of His coming again is the hope of the Church.

## Christ, Resurrection of

### Matt. xxviii. 1-10.

Seek God early (*v.* 1). Matt. vi. 33.
Let every morning remind us of Christ's coming, and Christ's resurrection (*v.* 1).
If help from earth fails us, God will send it from heaven (*v.* 3).
'Come' and get salvation, then 'go' and proclaim it (*vv.* 6, 7).
Christ wants practical, active servants (*v.* 8).
To hearts of love and hands of service, Christ is first revealed (*v.* 9).
No man can go on God's errands without His company (*v.* 9).
The world may boast of its titles. We who are called " His brethren " have the highest (*v.* 10).

## Christ's Trial before the High Priest

### Mark xiv. 53-64.

He was despised and rejected of men, Isaiah liii. 3.
*Solitary.* All forsook Him, and fled. Have we ever done so?
*Sinless.* Sought for evidence of wrong and found none. False witness, Matt. xxvi. 50. So since, in all centuries, men have sought arguments against Saviour, but have failed.
*Slandered.* False witness. The spirit of deception in the world. Fraudulent adulteration is a false witness.
*Silent.* He held His peace (*vv.* 60, 61). His life and doctrine was sufficient reply. Example to us of patience under calumny and false accusation.
*Speaking.* Jesus said, I am (*v.* 2). When our word is challenged, we may be patiently silent ; when God's word is assailed, then be bold to speak.
*Supreme* (*v.* 62). Christ's divine life was proof of His claim to Messiahship. He claimed to be God, and He lived like a God.
*Sentenced.* All condemned Him (*v.* 64). His death voluntary. His condemnation purchased our freedom. He was stripped that we might wear the robe of righteousness. He wore a crown of thorns that we might wear a crown of glory. He suffered, the just for unjust, that He might bring us to God.

### Christian's Gladness, A

Ps. xxxii. 11.

Its spring.    In the Lord.
Its vivacity.    Shout.
Its propriety.    It is commended.
Its beneficial results and its abundant reasons.
Upright in heart.    Not horizontal or grovelling, but vertical.

### Christian's Marks, A

Saving acquaintance *with* Christ (1 John iii. 5).
Surrender of will *to* Christ (1 John v. 14).
Sympathy with all the members o´Christ (1 John iii. 14).
Stedfast abiding *in* Christ (1 John iii. 6).
Successful in conflict *through* Christ (1 John ii. 13).
Seeking to act *like* Christ (1 John ii. 29).
Swayed by the Holy Spirit *for* Christ (1 John iii. 24).

### Christians as Lights

Phil. ii. 15.

*Privilege* to shine (Matt. v. 14 ; John viii. 12).
Light shines into them (Ps. cxix. 130).
Are called to shine (1 John i. 7).
*Responsibility.* Give out light (Matt. v. 15).
Not hide (Matt. v. 16).
For others (Acts xiii. 47).
Power.    Not self (Matt. v. 16).
Lightbearer (Phil. ii. 15).

### Christian's Resolve and Privilege

Ps. xxxiv. 1.

Firm resolution.    Serious difficulties in carrying it out.    Help for its performance.    Excellent consequence of so doing.
Six questions.    Who?    I.    What?    Will bless whom?    The Lord.    When?    At all times.    How? Why?
All answered form a direction for making a heaven below.

### Christian Confidence

*"My times are in Thy hands."*—Ps. xxxi. 15.

I. THE CHARACTER OF THE EARTHLY
EXPERIENCE OF SAINTS.

My times; that is, the changes I shall pass through.

II. THE ADVANTAGE OF THIS VARIETY.

Changes reveal the different aspects of the Christian character.
Changes strengthen character.
Changes lead us to admire the unchanging God.

III. COMFORT FOR ALL SEASONS.

Changes of life are subject to the divine control.
God will support His people under them, and as a result they will be abundantly profited.

IV. THE DEPORTMENT WHICH SHOULD
CHARACTERISE US.

Resignation and contentment.
Zeal and hope.

### Christian Work, Prosperity in

Neh. iii. and iv.

Chapter iii. A chapter of names but full of teaching. Building is begun.
All classes worked, as we see (*v.* 1).
Unity (*v.* 2).
Diversity (*v.* 9).
Individuality (*v.* 12).
Women took part (Phil. iv. 3).
No gaps. Each worked in own sphere.
Note three essential things—Chapter iv.

I. Working.
The people had a mind to work (*v.* 6).
Every one had his work to do (*v.* 15).
Extended service (*v.* 21).

II. Praying (*vv.* 4, 5, 9; 1 Thess. v. 17).

III. Watchfulness (*v.* 9). Set a watch.
Prayer without watching is impious to God, and watching without prayer is impious to ourselves.
Good counsel in difficulty (*v.* 14).
Secret of success (*v.* 20).

B

### Church's First Disciple

#### John i. 34.

1. Heralding of Christ. Baptist's ministry was brief—six months. Popular. Misunderstood. Expectant. Self-abnegating.

2. Manifestation of Christ in His true character and mission. John says, "Behold"—not the great teacher, or spotless example, or triumphant king, but—the "Lamb of God." Jesus says, "What seek ye?" an affectionate inquiry. "Come and see," an encouraging invitation.

3. Beginning of the Christian Church. By friendly service. Brotherly affection. Neighbourly zeal. Conquest of prejudice.

4. Result of personal effort. Industrial endeavours. Sabbath-school class may include a Wilberforce, or the audience a Spurgeon.


### Clean Heart, A

#### Ps. li. 10.

Purity to pray for. Hyssop, the lowliest of all Eastern plants. Blessing of a clean heart is included in Christ's redemption (Tit. ii. 14).

By the will of God (Dan. xii. 10 ; 1 Thess. iv. 3).

Through the atonement of Christ (Heb. ix. 14 ; 1 John i. 7).

By the Word of God (Eph. v. 25).

By the Holy Spirit (Rom. xv. 16).

By faith in Christ (Acts xv. 9).

To possess a clean heart is to have a submissive will.

A holy affection, a pure mind, and a love for God's Word.

A plea for mercy is a confession of guilt.

If we deal seriously with our sins, God will deal tenderly with us. The *necessity* of the sinner is the *opportunity* of the Saviour. The really penitent desire purity as well as pardon.

Sinful conception is an evil anterior to personal transgression.

Comfort always comes after cleansing.

He whose sins have been forgiven need never fear that they will be remembered again.

A rejoicing believer has power over men.

## Comfort in Adversity

### Ps. lvii. 3.

1. All contingencies are provided for. *He shall* (or will) *send.*
2. The highest sources are available "from heaven."
3. The worst foes will be overcome in the end.
4. By the holiest means, "mercy and truth."

## Commandments, Ten, Summarised

### Exod. xx.

1. Supreme love to God can have "no other gods."
2. Love resents every effort to represent its object as bird, or beast, or serpent.
3. Love never dishonours God's name by taking it in vain.
4. Love makes us reverence the "Lord's day."
5. Love makes home happy.
6. Love can never kill.
7. Lust, not love, breaks the Seventh Commandment.
8. Love prevents lying lips, love stops the voice of slander.
9. Love will give, but never steal.
10. Love has no covetous eyes for his neighbour's possession.

## Communion

" *The secret place of the Most High.*"—Ps. xci. 1.

God is everywhere, yet we never find Him till we enter the " secret place."
Christ is the secret place. With God from beginning. *Secret.* Love between Father and Son greater than we can fathom. Only seen when Holy Spirit opens our eyes. *Safety. Christ* the only Ark. *Rest.* Perfect love, perfect power, perfect glory. Here we find comfort in sorrow, hope in trouble, calmness in storm, strength in weakness.
*The Most High.* Its majesty shows our position; our calling, our hope.
Dwell. Abide out and in. Our Sanctuary Home Friend. Break-bread. Communion, a foretaste of heaven.

### Congregation of One, A

Acts viii. 26–40.

There may be good work for us in unlikely places (*v.* 26).

The soul winner has inward direction, and follows it (*v.* 29).

Caste goes when Christ comes (*v.* 30).

The gospel levels all distinction (*v.* 30).

Though all may not proclaim Christ in the streets to thousands, all may speak to one hungry soul in the desert (*v.* 30).

Mysteries are revealed to the meek (*v.* 31).

Better confess ignorance in humility, than conceal it through pride (*v.* 34).

Jesus is the beginning and end of all true preaching (*v.* 35).

Time and space are nothing to God (*v.* 39).

### Contrasts

Heed these things.    Shortness and length.

*Short—*
1. Life is very short (Ps. xxxix. 5; Jas. iv. 14).
2. Time is very short (1 Cor. vii. 29).
3. Sinners' joy is short (Job xxii. 16).
4. Saints' sorrow is short (2 Cor. iv. 17).

*Long—*
1. God Himself (Ps. xc. 2; 1 Tim. i. 17).
2. God's love (Ps. ciii. 17).
3. Life to come (John iii. 16).
4. Saints' joy (Ps. xvi. 11; Isa. xxxv. 10).
5. Sinners' sorrow (Isa. xxxiii. 14).

### Conversion

A radical change (2 Cor. v. 17).

A spiritual change (John iii. 6).

God's gift (Titus iii. 5).

Necessary (John iii. 3).

Commanded (Acts iii. 19).

Evidence (Matt. vii. 20).

Manner (Acts xvi. 31).

### Cross of Christ

Luke xxiii. 33, 46.

The Cross as a place of emptiness (Phil. ii. 7).

The Cross as a place of intercession (*v.* 34), Father forgive (*v.* 34).

The Cross a place of shame (Heb. xii. 3).

The Cross a place of seeming defeat (*v.* 35); obedience held Him (Phil. ii. 8) ; love held Him (Gal. ii. 20) ; joy held Him (Heb. xii. 2).

The Cross a place of self-sacrifice (*vv.* 37, 39).

The Cross a place of silence.

The Cross a place of mercy. Superscription in three languages : proclamation to *all* classes and conditions.

The Cross a place of power (*v.* 34).

The Cross a place of promise (*v.* 43).

The Cross a place of atonement (*v.* 45).

The Cross a place of justice (*v.* 46).

### Crowns, Seven

Crown of thorns. Curse for sin (Matt. xxvii. 29).

Crown of gold (Ps. xxi. 3 ; Rev. xiv. 14).

Crown of life. Reward of enduring temptation (Jas. i. 12).

Crown of incorruptibility. Reward of temperance (1 Cor. ix. 25).

Crown of righteousness. Reward of loving Christ's appearing (2 Tim. iv. 8).

Crown of rejoicing. Reward of soul winners (1 Thess. ii. 19).

Crown of glory. Reward of faithful ministry (Dan. xii. 3).

### Daniel's Influence
#### Dan. i.

Daniel prayed to his God.

Daniel purposed in his heart.

Daniel proposed to his partners.

Daniel plans for pulse.

Daniel pleads their claims.

All protected by the prince.

All pass the examination.

Pleasant faces.

Prominent places.

Permanent positions.

Proof positive for prohibition.

### Daniel, His Characteristics, a Study

Courteous (Dan. i. 8, 12).

Attractive (Dan. i. 4, 9).

Temperate (Dan. i. 8).

Studious (Dan. i. 17, 19).

Courageous (Dan. ii. 13-16; vi. 7, 11).
Humble (Dan. ii. 30 ; ix. 7, 20).
Faithful (Dan. vi. 4).
Bible student (Dan. ix. 2 ; xi. 13).
Prayerful (Dan. ii. 18 ; vi. 10; ix. 4; xii. 8).
Honoured (Dan. ii. 48 ; vi. 23 ; xii. 13).

### Daniel's Loyalty
Dan. vi.

Prayer and praise should go to heaven arm-in-arm
(v. 10).

The best characters are most tested (v. 16).

Our willingness to suffer is the test of our Christianity (v. 16).

Envy is sharper than a serpent's tooth (v. 17).

A guilty conscience makes a sleepless pillow (v. 18).

Better be in a den of lions with God, than out of
it serving Satan (v. 22).

Those who cheerfully trust God shall never be
ashamed of their confidence (v. 23).

The way of transgressors is hard (v. 24).

### David's Calling
Ps. lxxviii. 70, 71.

Two questions.

How was David's shepherd life an unconscious
preparation for his calling? How did the Divine
summons, when it came, fit him for his mighty destiny? He was sent back to his flocks. Two great
convictions awakened in him then, that proved in
him elements of strength. Learn—

The belief in a Divine leader (Ps. xxiii.).

The belief in a Divine choice.

Its modern lessons—

There is a Divine plan in every life.

There is a Divine vocation for every man.

There is a Divine Shepherd for every man.

### Dedicating the Temple
Ezra vi.

That Church will prosper whose teachers speak in-
spired truth (v. 1).

The way of prosperity is according to the commandment of God (v. 1).

No man who helps the people of God is forgotten
by God (v. 1).

Dedicate yourself to God for service, then dedicate your service to Him (*v.* 16).

It is a joy to build for the glory of God and the good of men (*v.* 16).

What belongs to God should be dedicated to Him (*v.* 17).

Only the pure can lead in God's worship (*v.* 20).

### Dorcas and Good Deeds
Acts ix. 36.

He is a saint who devotes himself to Christ as a peculiar servant (*v.* 32).

The true teacher draws away attention from himself to his Lord (*v.* 34).

No man was ever converted but his conversion affected some one else (*v.* 35).

The restoration of one may lead to the conversion of many (*v.* 35).

Good works come from the heart, and pass through the hands (*v.* 36).

The presence and prayers of a loving minister are precious in time of trouble (*v.* 38).

Acts of benevolence are the best relics (*v.* 39).

No house is low where a saint lives (*v.* 43).

### End of Life, The
Ps. xxxix. 4.

What we may desire to know about our end—not its date, place, circumstances, *but its nature.* Will it be the end of saint or sinner?

Its *certainty* and *nearness.*

Life's issues and requirements.

In the matter of attention, preparation, passport.

Why ask God to make us know it? Because the knowledge is important, difficult to acquire.

To keep its end in view, and be prepared.

### Esau's Birthright, Sale of
Gen. xxv. 31.

Brothers differed in appearance and character.

Birthright, Barter, Bitter Cry.

> No action, whether foul or fair,
> Is ever done, but it leaves somewhere
> A record, written by fingers ghostly,
> As a blessing or a curse, and mostly
> In the greater weakness or greater strength
> Of the acts which follow it, till at length
> The wrongs of ages are redressed,
> And the justice of God made manifest.

### Excuses, Hollow

The excuse of unbelief (John iii. 12).
The excuse of fear (Luke xix. 11–27).
The excuse of procrastination (Acts xxiv. 22–27).
The excuse of false modesty (Num. xiii. 26–33).
The excuse of other business (Luke xiv. 16–24).
Therefore make no excuses (John iv. 31–38).
Will our excuses stand? (Acts xxvi. 19–28).

### Faith a Shield

Ps. v. 12.

Shield not a defence for any particular part. Other armour has each its own design. Shield defends the whole man. Skilfully used to preserve and cover all. It keeps the arrow from helmet as well as head, from the breast and breastplate. Faith is thus armour upon armour, a grace that preserves all other graces.

A sense of Divine favour, a defence to the soul.

### Faith and Unbelief

*Report of the spies.*—Num. xiii. 17–33.

Faith bears fruit—unbelief is barren (*vv.* 26, 27).
Faith looks up (*v.* 30). Unbelief looks around (*v.* 29).
Faith says, " We were well able " (*v.* 30). Unbelief says, " We be not able " (*v.* 31).
Faith magnifies God (*v.* 30). Unbelief magnifies difficulties (*v.* 32).
Faith brings a good report, unbelief an evil report (*v.* 32).
Faith sees God, unbelief sees giants (*vv.* 28–33).
Faith takes us into Canaan (Heb. iv. 3). Unbelief shuts us out (Heb. iii. 19).

### Faith by, and in Faith

Access by faith (Rom. v. 2).
Justified by faith (Rom. v. 1).
Live by faith (Gal. ii. 20).
Walk by faith (2 Cor. v. 7).
Sanctified by faith (Acts xxvi. 18).
Purified by faith (Acts xv. 9).
Ask in faith (Jas. i. 6).
Resist in faith (1 Pet. v. 9).
Boldness in faith (1 Tim. iii. 13).
Continue in faith (1 Tim. ii. 15).
Rich in faith (James ii. 5).
Died in faith (Heb. xi. 13).

### Faith, Seven types of

Abel—justifying faith (Heb. xi. 4).
Enoch—sanctifying faith (Heb. xi. 15).
Noah—separation of faith (Heb. xi. 7).
Abraham—obedient faith (Heb. xi. 8).
Isaac—patient faith (Heb. xi. 20).
Jacob—suffering faith (Heb. xi. 21).
Joseph—victorious faith (Heb. xi. 22).

### Fear of Natural Death

1 Cor. xv. 55-57.

Physical weaknesses (Matt. viii. 17).
Sorrows (Rev. xxi. 4).
Care (1 Pet. v. 7).
Worrying and fretting (Isa. xxvi. 3).
Ignorance (Jas. i. 5).
False doctrines (John vii. 17).
Forgetfulness (John xiv. 26).

### Fear Nots of the Bible

(Isa. xliii. 1 ; Isa. li. 11 ; Heb. xii. 28 ; Exod. xx. 20 ; Isa. xii. 2 ; Hag. ii. 5 ; Mal. ii. 5 ; Matt. x. 20 ; Rev. i. 17).

### Feeding the Five Thousand

Mark vi. 30-44.

Those who preach will pray much (v. 30).
They who serve much in public need to be much with God in private (v. 31).
Without quiet hours we shall grow faint or formal (v. 31).
Our poverty brings out His riches (v. 37).
Orderly arrangement is a good handmaiden (v. 39).
Positions of difficulty are places of blessing (v. 41).
God uses human instrumentality to supply human need. Is He using you?
Whom Christ feeds He fills (v. 42).
Those who would be charitable must be provident (v. 42).
We get by giving (v. 43).
A little with God's blessing will feed many (v. 44).

### Fishers of Men

Mark iv. 19.

Jesus, the greatest, links Himself with the lowest Fisher disciples.
Follow Me, and I will make you fishers of men.

Cannot be useful unless we are used.

Note how Jesus fished, and imitate Him.

He always went to the *right place*.

Always go at the *right time*.   Some fish are best caught at sunlight, others in shadow.

Always in the *right way*.   153 different species of fish.   Some by hook, some by net, spear, and harpoon.

Adapt your ways of working.

Choose the *right bait*.   Word of God.

Exercise patience.

### Fishers of Men (for Workers)

#### Mark i. 17.

Christ called two disciples zealous in their work. Fishers now, I will make you fishers of men.

A fisherman must be acquainted with the sea.   So study human nature, its character, disposition.   A true fisherman must know how to allure fish.   Torches burned at night.   Fish attracted by the glare, others by ground bait.   Study pursuits, habits, and lives of people.   Use tact.

A fisherman must possess patience.   Toiled all night and caught nothing.   So Sunday School Teacher must toil.   Tract distributer plod on. Minister, preach and labour.

A fisherman must run hazards.   Treacherous sea, the Lake of Galilee.   So whenever called and wherever, we must go.   Brave heart and firm faith wanted.

A fisherman must know how to persevere and expect.   At Christ's bidding, after a night of toil, they launched out.   Sow the seed beside all waters.

Work, Wait, and Pray.

### Friendship

#### 1 Sam. xviii. 1.

Jews have proverb that a man without friends is like the left hand without the right.

Faithful friend one of earth's greatest blessings.

Duties are reciprocal.

1. Jonathan and David's friendship.   Very strong. Disinterested.   Very ardent, constant, faithful, based on true piety.

2. Was a type of great love which Christ has for every believer.   All love is a type of His love.

Like as a father, etc.   He loved us and sought us.

Jonathan entered into covenant.   *So* Jesus is with us, for this life and life to come.

### "Fruit" in the Season
Ps. i. 3 ; Gal. v. 22.

When is "the season" for—
Love—when hated (Matt. v. 44).
Joy—in trial (Jas. i. 2).
Peace—the storm (Ps. xlvi. 1-3).
Longsuffering—when injured (1 Cor. xiii. 7).
Gentleness—when opposed (2 Tim. ii. 24).
Goodness—in time of need (Isa. lviii. 6, 7).
Faithfulness—when many are failing (Matt. xxiv. 12).
Meekness—when reviled (1 Pet. ii. 23).
Self-control—when eating and drinking (1 Cor. x. 31).
Temperance—in good things, and total abstinence from evil (1 Thess. v. 22).
How much fruit? (Phil i. 11).

### Fulness of Joy
Ps. xvi. 11.

Quality—there are pleasures.
Quantity—fulness.
Dignity—at God's right hand.
Duration—for evermore.

### Gambling, Evils of

*Definition.* Obtaining money, or money's worth, without giving an equivalent.
*Results.* 1. Sees neighbour possessing property, and covets it.
2. Deliberately sets himself to rob or ruin.
3. Pleasure of gambling is the pleasure of gain without toil or earning it.
4. Pleasure is a delusion, so also is the profit.
5. Gambling robs men of all character, and is an inlet to *all* other vices.
6. The gambler is a moral pestilence, for by his acts he leads others to ruin.

### God is a Sun and Shield
Ps. lxxxiv. 11.

The sun gives light (Ps. cxix. 130).
The sun gives health (Ps. xlii. 11).
The sun centre of attraction (John xii. 32).
The sun centre of all physical power (Matt. xxviii. 18; Acts i. 8).

**As a Shield.** A defence for all the other armour. It diverts the arrow from helmet as well as from head, from the breastplate as well as the heart. Shield of faith (Eph. vi. 16). Armour upon armour.

### God's Goodness to Man
#### Ps. lxxiii. 1.
Israel's receipts from God are—
For quantity, the greatest.
For variety, the choicest.
For quality, the sweetest.
For security, the surest.
For duration, the most lasting.

### God's Judgments
#### Ps. xxxvi. 6.
*Are often unfathomable.* We cannot discover the foundation, cause, or spring.
*They are safe sailing.* Ships never strike on rocks in the great deeps.
*They conceal* great treasure, and work great good. Great deep, not a salt and barren wilderness, is one of the greatest blessings to the world.
*Becomes a highway* of communion with God.

### God's People are Called
Believers (1 Tim. iv. 12).
Christians (1 Pet. iv. 16).
Saints (Eph. iii. 18).
Brethren (Heb. ii. 11).
Sons of God (1 John iii. 2).
Friends (John xv. 14).
Sheep (John x. 14).

### God's Word
Enduring (Isa. xl. 8 ; 1 Pet. i. 25).
Life-giving (John vi. 63, 68).
Healing (Ps. cvii. 20 ; Matt. viii. 8).
Discerning (Heb. iv. 12).
Profitable (2 Tim. iii. 16).
Nourishing (1 Tim. iv. 6 ; 1 Pet. ii. 2).
Comforting (1 Thess. iv. 18).

### Golden Chain of Thirteen Links
1. Hear the best men, read the best books, keep the best company.
2. Meditate often on the four last things.    Death

which is most certain; Judgment, which is most
strict; Hell, which is most doleful; Heaven, which
is most delightful.

3. Be willing to want what God is not willing to
give.

4. Do you bless God most when you are most
blessed.

5. Fear not the fear of men.

6. Acquaint yourselves with yourselves.

7. Improve that time which will be yours but for
a time.

8. Learn humility from Christ's humility.

9. Be upright Christians.

10. Take nothing upon trust, but all upon trial.

11. Take those reproofs which you need most.

12. Live in love, and live in truth.

13. Set out with God at the beginning, and hold
out with God until your ending.—*Dyer.*

### Good Desire, A

Rom. x. 1–4.

1. *A title which should never be forgotten:*
"*Brethren.*" Division in Christian fellowship is
disruption of Christian force.

2. *A marriage which none should divorce.* "My
heart's desire and prayer to God." If desires right,
then prayer will be real.

3. *A patriotism above suspicion.*

4. *A need which is most imperative.* "That they
might be saved." (See Phil. iii. 8, 9.)

5. *An earnestness which may be an error.* "Zeal
of God, but not according to knowledge."

6. An ignorance which is quite inexcusable.
"Ignorant of God's righteousness."

7. *An effort which must always be a failure.*
"Establish our own righteousness." Self-righteousness is a stumbling-block.

8. *An obstinacy which must end in ruin.* Submission, self-surrender, salvation.

9. *A direction which is simple and certain.*
"Christ the end of the law," etc.

10. A *sine quâ non* of salvation. Truth and mercy
must meet.

11. *An opportunity abundantly open for all.*
"Every one that believeth."

12. A means eminently simple to salvation; sub-
limely sure and glorious.

### Good Samaritan and Christ

Luke x. 25-37.

He came where he was. Jesus "came" down.

He had compassion on him. Includes salvation.

He bound up his wounds. Healed the broken-hearted.

He set him on his own beast. Jesus took our place.

He provided for him during his absence, and Jesus commended us to His Father (John xvii. 11).

He left money to sustain him. Jesus left us His Holy Spirit and the Word.

He promised to come again (John xiv. 1-3; 2 Tim. iv. 8).

### Good Shepherd

John x. 11-18.

Bible Shepherd (Gen. xlvii. 3 ; Luke ii. 8).

Lord my Shepherd (Ps. xxiii.).

He knows His sheep (John x. 14).

He provides for them (John x. 9).

He guides them (Prov. viii. 28).

He gives His life (John x. 15).

He delights in them (1 Pet. ii. 9).

### Gospel, A Full

Rom. i. 16.

Key-note to the epistle—

Justification by faith introduced (Rom. i.).

Sanctification by the Spirit (Rom. viii. 1).

Consecration for service (Rom. xii. 1).

Essentials and theme—

Jesus Living, our Example (1 Pet. ii. 21).

Jesus Dying, our Redeemer (Tit. ii. 14).

Jesus Buried, our Scapegoat (Lev. xvi. 21).

Christ Risen, our Justifier (Rom. iv. 25).

Christ Ascended, our Head (Col. i. 18).

Christ Coming, our Hope (Tit. ii. 13).

### Gospel Harvest

Ps. lxxii. 16.

A handful of corn—the gospel.

The places where it is sown.

The effect which the gospel, when thus sown, will produce in the world.

As merchants carry small sample bags of grain, so you carry some. When you write, drop a word in the letter. The most difficult place, the steepest mountain, the least hopeful place often proves the most fruitful.

### Gospel Invitation
#### Isa. lv. 1-8.

*Accept.* (*v.* 1.)
*Loud.* Ho ! Great way off.
*Personal.* Every one.
*Abounding* Waters. Not a drop but running fountain.
*Generous.* Wine and Milk. God offers not only necessaries, but luxuries (Isa. xxv. 6).
*Free.* Without money.
(*v.* 7.) Abundant *pardon.*
*Love* passing knowledge (Eph. iii. 18, 19).
Abundant *means.*
Abundant *sins.* More than the sands.
Abundant *ease.* Come and take and eat.
Abundant *fulness.* Sins past and present and future (*v.* 3).

### Gospel Invitation
#### Isa. lv. 1-12.

1. We come to the waters, but find wine and milk. (*v.* 8).
2. Another moment may place us beyond the reach of pardon (*v.* 6).
3. If redeemed, we desire others to come to " our God " (*v.* 7).
4. We cannot have God's thoughts whilst filled with our own opinions (*v.* 8).
5. God's way will be clear when we get to the end of our own (*v.* 9).
6. Nothing is wasted in God's House (*v.* 10).
7. God-sent messages never go to the dead letter office (*v.* 11).
8. A great hallelujah chorus awaits the return of God's people (*v.* 12).

### Gospel, Power of the
#### Rom. i. 8-17.

Prayer should be constant, definite, and submissive (*vv.* 8-10).
None so poor he may not impart to us something of value (*v.* 12).

Our debt to others can never be paid but in faithful service to Christ (*v.* 14).

Sending the gospel to the heathen is paying a debt of love (*v.* 14).

Be ready for every opportunity of doing good (*v.* 15).

We should neither be ashamed of the gospel nor a shame to it (*v.* 16).

The power of the gospel is the confidence of its preachers (*v.* 16).

We are made righteous before God, not by what we do, but believing what God in Christ has done (*v.* 17).

The cross reveals God's righteousness and His wrath (*vv.* 17, 18).

### Gospel, The

Gospel plan is—

Admit God, submit to God, commit to God, transmit from God to others.

### Grace, Described and Pourtrayed

The Bread of Life seeking the hungry.
The Living Water seeking the thirsty.
The Garments of Salvation seeking the naked.
The Truth seeking the liar.
The Rest seeking the weary.
The Light seeking the darkness.
The Pardon seeking the guilty.
Mercy seeking the wretched.
Life seeking death.

### Grace of God, The

Tit. ii. 11-14.

Its manifestation. " Hath appeared " to all men.
Its work. " Bringing salvation " to all.

Teaching us—

Its purpose. To help us to " deny ungodliness and worldly lusts," to " live soberly, righteously, and godly in this present world "; to teach us to look " for that blessed hope, and glorious appearing of Jesus Christ."

### Great Revival, A

Neh. i.

The state of Zion. Affliction and reproach.

The inward preparation for a great change ; weeping, fasting, praying (*v.* 4).

Note the prayer (*vv.* 5 to 11).
Reverent (*v.* 5).
Persistent (*v.* 6).
Penitent (*v.* 7).
Scriptural (*v.* 8).
Child-like (*v.* 10).
Definite (*v.* 11).     (See Ps. cxlv. 19.)

### Harvest Time
Matt. xiii. 19.

*Proclaims God's faithfulness.* While the earth remaineth, seed time, etc., shall not cease (Gen. viii. 22).
*Tells of God's goodness.* Thou crownest the year with goodness, etc. (Ps. lxv. 11, 13).
*A time for prayer and work.* Harvest great (Matt. ix. 37, 38).
*A time of joy* (Isa. ix. 3).     Returning bearing sheaves (Ps. cxxvi. 6).
*A testing time* (Matt. xiii. 30).
*Is connected with seed time* (Gal. vi. 7, 8).
*Speaks loudly to unsaved* (Jer. viii. 20).

### Harvest Time
Gen. viii. 22.

God's law as to sowing (Gen. i. 12).
In kind, quality, and quantity, we reap as we sow (Gal. vi. 8).
Salvation is of grace.   Reward according to works (1 Cor. ix. 24, 25).
Life is in Christ.   The race and crown to be won (1 Cor. ix. 24, 25).
Jacob sowed deceit and reaped deception, exile and wandering (Gen. xxvii. 24).
His sons sold Joseph, and they became slaves for 400 years.
Saul sowed disobedience, lost his kingdom and life (1 Sam. xiii. 13).
Reject God's truth, and reap a harvest of lies through eternity (Rev. xxii. 15).

### Harvest Time and its Lessons

What riches earth has thrown up from her bosom. The wealth of harvest.
The husbandman enjoys anticipated harvest in prospect ; no sight so lovely as the beauty of harvest.

C

Golden Reapers' song.    Sharpening of sickle.
Music of the harvest.

Patient waiting, submission to Heavenly influences,
reaching Godward, reflecting as best we can the
golden glory of the King of the skies, and bowing
to the sickle at last.

### Heaven, Recognition of Friends in

A belief in this doctrine has a tendency to elevate,
strengthen and purify our earthly affections.
Induces us to form proper friendships here.
Brings us more strongly under the power of
heavenly realities and attractions.
Consoling to those suffering bereavement.

### Heaven, Representation of

As a Kingdom (Matt. xviii. 1-4).
As a City (Rev. xxii. 2-5).
As a Home (John xiv. 2 ; Eph. iii. 15).
As a Rest (Heb. iv. 9 ; Rev. xiv. 13).
As an Inheritance (Col. i. 12 ; 1 Pet. i. 3-5).

### Heavenly Inheritance

1 Pet. i. 1-12.

Grace is the source of peace (*v*. 2).
The highest ground of praise is the gift of God
(*v*. 3).
Mercy for our misery, grace for our guilt (*v*. 3).
The resurrection of Christ was the birth of Christ
(*v*. 3).
Our inheritance is in substance *incorruptible*, in
purity *undefiled*, in beauty *unfading*, in durability
*everlasting* (*v*. 4).
Afflictions are only sent when we need them
(*v*. 6).
We must be proved before we can be approved
(*v*. 7).
Faith begets love, and both give assurance. If
Christ Is so much to us unseen, what will He be
when we see Him? (*v*. 8).
Will you neglect what prophets and apostles and
angels searched into? (*vv*. 11, 12).

### Heavenly Riches

Riches of His *Goodness* (Rom. ii. 4). God's out-
ward manifestation in nature, in the rain, sunshine,
flowers and fruit.

Riches of His *Grace* (Eph. i. 7). Where sin abounded, grace much more abounded (Rom. v.) ; "much more " used six times.

Riches of *Glory* (Eph. iii. 16). Riches of grace come from the Cross ; riches of glory from the throne. These riches to be greatly strengthened with might by His Spirit in the inner man.

That Christ may dwell in your hearts as source of life and sustenance of life.

### Heavenly Vision, The

" *Whereupon, O King Agrippa, I was not dis-obedient to the heavenly vision.*"—Acts xxvi. 19.

1. The heavenly vision was a revelation of self and of sin.
2. A revelation of Christ.
3. A revelation of duty.
4. Its effect upon character.
5. The life of him who is thus obedient.
6. The objections of those who endeavour to measure eternal issues by temporal standards.
7. "I am Jesus, whom thou persecutest."

### Help of God for His own Cause Pleaded

" *Arise, O God! plead Thine own cause.*"—Is. lxxiv. 22.

God has a cause in our world.

It is distinguished by certain striking characteristics. Its knowledge, holiness, and benevolence.

Though God's cause comprises many elements, it is yet one. It is greatly impeded and opposed.

Prayer to God on behalf of His cause is the Church's duty.

God can and will most effectually answer the prayer of His people.

Then—
Who are with Christ in this cause?
Who are indifferent and opposed to it?

### " He Shalls," Seven

He shall deliver (Ps. xci. 3).
He shall cover (Ps. xci. 4).
He shall give (Ps. xci. 11 ; xxxvii. 4).
He shall bring (Ps. xxxvii. 5, 6).
He shall teach (John xiv. 26).
He shall direct (Prov. iii. 6).
He shall guide (John xvi. 13).

### High Living

*" The just shall live by faith."*—Rom. i. 17.

This is a gem from Habakkuk.  Paul found this jewel in Habakkuk's casket.

Christian life summarized.  Faith is the Christian's vital principle, his life-germ.

Faith is the actuating principle and soul force of the Christian life.

It is to be in continual operation from first to last.

Is intensely practical, exclusive of every other principle that may compete with it.

Applicable to all kinds of living.  Whether high or lower plane of life, ordinary and common-place, or exalted and heroic, long or short, or at its highest pitch, it is to be lived by faith.

Live this life in prayer.  Personally.  I sought the Lord, and He heard *me.*

Live it by faith in the Son of God.

### Holy Spirit, Office and Work of

To strive (Acts vii. 51).
To send forth (John xv. 26).
To move (Gen. i. 2).
To speak (John xvi. 13).
To guide (John xvi. 13).
To lead (Rom. viii. 14).
To help (Rom. viii. 26).
To search (1 Cor. ii. 10).
To prophesy (John xvi. 13).
To intercede (Rom. viii. 26).
To sanctify (1 Cor. vi 11).
To work in soul (1 Cor xii. 11).

### Home Gathering (a Christmas Thought)

1 Sam. xx. 6.

Time-honoured custom in Jesse's family.

Christmas emphasises the reunion and joys of home.  Varieties of affection in our household.

Father for a child.  Gratitude, love for helpless infancy, pride in possibilities of the child.

Love of a mother.  Her own life and the new life, giving unlimited expression, pitying and loving even what the world counts worthless.

Love of children for parents.  Slow growth hidden at first by weeds of wilfulness.

In childhood a compend of gratitude, reverence and trust.

Love between brothers and sisters.  Dependence.

Sharing toys and table, intertwining sympathies and affections. Manliness in brothers, gentle beauty in the sisters.

### Human Life and Spiritual Existence

Triple alliance.
Bodily needs—food, warmth, light.
Mental needs—true and beautiful.
Spiritual needs—peace of conscience and the good.
Satisfaction of bodily needs gives us pleasure.
Satisfaction of mental needs gives us happiness.
Satisfaction of spiritual needs gives us bliss.

### "I Wills"—Resolution—Seven

I will pray (Ps. cxxi. 1).   I will go (Ps. lxxi. 16).
I will trust (Isa. xii. 2).   I will pay (Ps. cxvi. 14, 18).
I will praise (Ps. xxxiv.   I will hope (Ps. lxxi. 14).
1).
I will take (Ps. cxvi. 13).

### Jacob at Bethel

Gen. xxviii. 10–22.

From our greatest trials spring our choicest blessings.
Wherever we are, in city, shop, street or field, it is our fault if we do not keep up our intercourse with heaven (*v.* 11).
The pathway opened for sinful man is straight into God's presence (*v.* 12).
God is the source of all blessings.
If the angels come down with mercies, we must send them back with praises.
Those are safe whom God protects, whoever pursues them (*v.* 15).
Every house of God is a gate of heaven to the true worshipper (*v.* 17).
When God meets us with special presence, we ought to meet Him with humble reverence (*v.* 16).

### Jacob's Prayer

Gen. xxxii. 9.

No man need ever despair because of past misdoing (*v.* 9).
The best we can say to God is what He has said of us (*v.* 9).

We are prepared for great mercies when we see ourselves unworthy of the least (*v.* 10).

Wrong-doing brings fear and failure (*v.* 11).

A time of fear should be a time of prayer (*v.* 11).

The world's threats should drive us to God's promises (*v.* 12).

Keep a record in a blank book of each promise, prayer and answer. It will help you to praise and glorify God.

Prayer does not change God; it prepares us to receive what we ask (*v.* 28).

Power with God for men ensures power with men for God (*v.* 28).

### Jacob's Resolve

Gen. xxviii.

Study God's dealings with Jacob.

He revealed Jacob to himself.

He permitted Jacob to suffer loss of all earthly friends and goods.

He thrust into Jacob's life a revelation of His love.

It will make us quick to discover God and inspire godly fear, constrain us to give ourselves to Him, to devote our property to Him, and will fill us with joy.

### Jehovah's Goodness

Ps. ciii.

God's *all* cannot be praised with less than our *all*.

Not to thank God for mercies is to forget them.

Forgiveness is grounded in the grace of God, not in the worth of man.

A crown of glory is the favour of God.

A worldling may be satiated, but only a Christian can be satisfied.

Trust God, and you will find that He has no favourites.

Above the mountains of our sins the floods of God's mercy rise.

God bears no grudge.

It is impossible for forgiven sin to come back upon the soul.

Forgiveness is the greatest proof of love.

God's mercy is better than life, for it will outlive it

### Jesus Christ, Birth of
#### Luke ii. 11.

The world's first gift to Jesus was a manger, its last a cross (*v.* 7).

When ambitious for a high place remember the Master's cradle (*v.* 7).

Revelations are never made to idle men (*v.* 8).

The greatest blessings may come in the performance of daily toil (*v.* 8).

Gladness is the key-note of the gospel (*v.* 10).

The coming of Christ is the greatest event in history (*v.* 11).

Jesus is Saviour by covenant, Christ by commission, and Lord by right (*v.* 11).

Those who proclaim Jesus rank with the angels (*v.* 13).

God can get no higher glory than comes to Him through the work of Christ (*v.* 14).

Everything we have we owe to God's goodwill.

### Jesus, as High Priest
#### Zech. iii. 1-10.

When we stand before God we must expect the accusations of Satan (*v.* 1).

God's grace is our guarantee of heaven (*v.* 2).

If God plucks us out of the fire, Satan can never put us back again (*v.* 2).

The polluted may be purified (*v.* 4).

Holiness (*v.* 5) is the highway to happiness (*v.* 10).

Justification is not an excuse for sin, but a reason for obedience (*v.* 7).

If we will walk in God's ways He will show us the places to walk in (*v.* 7).

Angelic guidance is for the faithful (*v.* 7).

The greatness of our sin magnifies the greatness of God's mercy (*v.* 8).

The atonement of Christ is perfect, and needs no addition of penances (*v.* 9).

Christianity brings peace and prosperity to men individually and collectively (*v.* 10).

### Jesus, Temptation of
#### Matt. iv. 1-11.

Never go into a place of temptation (*v.* 1).

Know that it is no sin to be tempted.

See the necessity for temptation (*v.* 1). For proof, for usefulness, and for God's glory.

Cunningness of Satan.   Note the time, and he
begins with a doubt.
Resist the temptation.
Fight the devil with the sword of the Spirit.
Always trust God, but do not tempt Him.
Rightly divide the word (*v.* 6).

### Jesus, Voices of

Shepherd's Voice.   Follow Me.
Master's Voice.   Occupy.
Saviour's Voice.   Come unto Me.
Teacher's Voice.   Learn of Me.
Bridegroom's Voice.   Open to Me.
Friend's Voice.   Counsel thee.
Physician's Voice.   Wilt thou be made whole?

### Job, a Study
#### Job v.

*As a man.*   Not an imaginary man.   God says,
" There was a man."
*A perfect man.*   Upright.   Feared God and
eschewed evil.
*Sorely beset.*   Varied trials.
*Triumphant* man.   Conquered temptation.
Count him happy whom God correcteth (*v.* 17).
*Despise not chastening.*   It is the will of God
for us.
*Afflictions* teach us God's goodness.
Deliverance.   Freedom from fear.
Peace.   Freedom from sin.
Preparation for heaven.

### Job's appeal to God
#### Job xxiii. 1–10.

All desire for God is from God (*v.* 3).
Our deep desire to find God is met in Jesus Christ
(*v.* 3).
It matters little what man says of me, if I know
how God judges me (*v.* 5).
He is not far from God who has meditations of
Him in his heart (*v.* 6).
There is no flying from God's justice but in flying to
His mercy (*v.* 7).
Those delivered to God as their Owner will be
delivered from God as their Judge (*v.* 7).
It is a joy, when misunderstood, to know God sees
our inmost soul (*v.* 10).
Real religion will bear any test (*v.* 10).

### Justification, The Benefits of

#### Rom. v. 1–11.

*Peace.* Peace *with* God, *of* God. Unity of reconciliation (*v.* 1).

*Access* (*v.* 2). Not only reconciled, but admitted to His presence (Eph. ii. 3).

*Grace.* Called by (Gal. i. 15). Believe through (Acts xviii. 27). Grow in (2 Pet. iii. 18). Good Hope (2 Thess. ii. 16).

*Patience* (*v.* 3). Endurance, continuance. A disposition to suffer whatever pleases God.

*Experience* (*v.* 4). Patience in tribulation proves us (James v. 11).

*Hope* (*v.* 4). Contrast Job viii. 14 and Hebrews vi. 19.

*Joy in God* (*v.* 11). Gratitude to God brings delight in God Himself.

### Law and Grace

#### Rom. iii. 23, 24.

|  |  |
|---|---|
| Law says—Pay all. | Grace—All is paid. |
| Law is a work to do. | Grace is a work done. |
| Law restrains practice. | Grace changes principle. |
| Law speaks to servants. | Grace to sons and daughters. |
| Law points out defects. | Grace corrects them. |
| Law—Forgive, or you'll not be forgiven (Mark xi. 26). | Grace—Forgive as you have been forgiven (Eph. iv. 32). |
| Law—a lot of ceremonies. | Grace is actual experience. |
| Law is a yoke of bondage. | Grace is perfect liberty in the Spirit. |
| Law of sin and death. | Grace of love and life. |

### Law of Liberty

#### Jas. i. 25.

Look *reverently.* Same word in Greek as described John at early dawn seeking Christ at the open sepulchre.

Look *humbly.* Stoop and become as a little child, that you may learn.

Look *intently.* Search as men look for gold or gems.

Look thoughtfully.   Examine carefully.
Look understandingly.   It delivers from punish
ment of sin and slavery of sin.

### "Let us"

#### In Hebrews.

Fear (iv. 1).
Give diligence (iv. 11).
Hold fast (iv. 14).
Draw near (iv. 16 ; x. 22).
Go on unto perfection (vi. 1).
Consider one another (x. 24).
Lay aside (xii. 1).
Run (xii. 2).
Have grace (xii. 28).
Go forth unto Him (xiii. 13).
Offer the sacrifice of praise (xiii. 15).

### Life in Christ

#### John i. 4.

Christ is the source of life as Creator.   True in
widest sense.   He is Creator, not by delegation, but
as Principle.   This claim He vindicated in miracles.
He is the Redeemer of human existence.
Rational explanation of His death.   Redemption
is by price and power.
Man's true life consists in his union with Christ.
No true human life apart from God.
We forfeited life by sin, but recover it by Christ.

### Life's Work

#### John xvii. 4.

It is work that glorifies God.   Each one has his
proper work assigned him of God.
This work must be finished on earth.
To have finished this work is the most consolatory
deathbed reflection.
If called to our account, could we say, " Lord, here
is my life work.   Thou didst send me into the
world with a handful of seeds, and here is my heart
like a garden full of flowers "?

## Light at Eventide

*"At evening time it shall be light."*—Zech. xiv. 6, 7.

Truth suggested, upon surveying the past and the forecast of the future.

1. The old dispensation characterized by a conflict between powers of light and darkness. The Light of the World came in the Star of Bethlehem. Christ is the world's light.

By revealing to man himself, as he actually is and as he possibly may be.

By revealing to man, God as He is in contradistinction to man's previous conception of Him.

2. New dispensation is a conflict between light, as in Christ, and darkness, as in world.

In the individual.

In the world.

Realize now Christians, by His grace, are the light of the world. "Let your light so shine."

## Lily, Growth of a

Hosea xiv. 5.

Flowers are called stars of the earth.

Physical and moral blessings.

Consider the lilies (Matt. vi. 28).

True language of flowers speak of God's goodness.

Flowers adorn the bride and bedeck the chamber of mourning. Cheer the sick, and brighten and beautify the green carpet of the world.

1. The lily grows in silence. Love consistently.
2. The lily grows in beauty. Don't mar life.
3. The lily grows in purity. Youth, white blossom of a blameless life.

## Lord's Supper

Mark xiv. 12, 26.

1. The Passover (*v.* 12). Christ our Passover.
2. The Prayer. "Where wilt Thou that we go?" (*v.* 12). When in doubt where to work or how, ask Jesus. In Him you will find pleasant companionship (*v.* 13), implicit directions (*v.* 14), a prepared place (*v.* 15), real service (*v.* 16), the Lord's presence (*v.* 17).
3. The preparation (1 Cor. xi. 20).
4. The pain. Sorrowful (*vv.* 18, 19). Betrayed.
5. The praise. Bread was blessed (*v.* 22). Jesus,

knowing the agony, scourges, thorns, thirst, anguish,
the Father's averted face, yet praised God.

6. The participation. The sympathy, all drank.
The symbols, bread and wine, the supper, the song.

7. The purpose. This do (Luke xxii. 19).

### Lost Found, The (the Prodigal Son)

#### Luke xv. 11-24.

Wanted his own way, instead of father's will
(*v*. 12).

Heart gone, he follows (*v*. 13).

Spent all. Got all the world could give, and found
himself in want (*v*. 14).

Exchanged service of father for the enemy (*v*. 15).

Would not live with brother, but compelled to live
with swine (*v*. 15).

He had to come to himself before he came to the
father (*v*. 17).

His *will* took him *away*, his *want* brought him
*back* (*v*. 18).

Went out an heir, glad to return as beggar (*v*. 19).

Love is far-sighted. Saw son, not rags (*v*. 20).

Kiss first, confession next (*v*. 20).

Clothed first, then communion (*v*. 22).

### Love Expressed

#### John xii. 3.

No sacrifice is too costly or too mean tor Christ.

The incident reveals the insight of love.

The deed revealed the burden of a heart laden with
gratitude.

The Master estimates the deed at its true worth.

Personal love for a personal Saviour is the secret of
salvation and service. Saviour, Sovereign, Friend.

### The Lord is my Shepherd

#### Ps. xxiii.

*The deep consciousness that pervades it.* God is a
living, personal agent, who touches our life at every
point. The Lord is his Shepherd. He makes him
to lie down. He restores his soul. He leadeth in
paths of righteousness. He is with him in the valley.
His mercy follows him, and in His house he shall
find his home at last.

*The relation of God to the individual life.* My and

me occur in every line.  Close relation.  My Shepherd, my King, my God, my Rock, my High Tower, my Salvation.  Doctrine of special providence.  The happiness of the man whose God is the Lord, and it enables that man to look hopefully into the future.

Two things necessary if we would have this experience—

We must be reconciled to God.

We must be regenerated and renewed in our spirit.

### Lord our Refuge, The

*" The Lord is my strength and my shield."*—Ps. xxviii. 7.

### I. THE LORD ACKNOWLEDGED.

1. As the source of strength.
    (a) Physical.  (b) Intellectual.  (c) Spiritual.
2. As a shield.

Against temptation, the fiery darts of Satan, and the attacks of personal enemies.

### II. THE LORD TRUSTED.

1. With the heart.
2. For the salvation of the soul.
3. For the power to keep from falling.
4. For help in every hour of need.

### III. THE LORD REJOICED IN.

1. Because the soul is at peace with God.
2. Because of the consciousness of security in God.
3. Because of the manifested presence of God in the soul.

### IV. THE LORD PRAISED.

1. For the manifestation of His power.
    (a) To give strength in the hour of weakness.
    (b) To give encouragement in the hour of despondency.
    (c) To give light in the hour of darkness.
    (d) To give inspiration in the hour of conflict.
2. For the manifestation of His love.
    (a) In cleansing the heart from all sin.
    (b) In inscribing the name in heaven.
    (c) In the adoption of sons into the Divine family.
    (d) In the blessed assurance of an eternal home in heaven.

### Lord's Prayer Paraphrased

Matt. vi. 9.

Our Father. By right of creation, by bountiful provision, by gracious adoption.

Who art in heaven. Throne of glory, temple of angels.

Hallowed be Thy Name. By thoughts of our hearts, words of our lips, and work of our hands.

Thy kingdom come. Of providence to defend us, grace to refine us, glory to crown us.

Thy will be done, etc., toward us without resistance, by us without compulsion, universally, without exception.

Give us this day, etc., of necessity for our bodies, of eternal life for our soul.

Forgive us our trespasses, etc., against commands of thy law, against grace of the gospel.

As we forgive, etc., by defacing our characters, by embezzling our property.

Lead us not, etc., of overwhelming affliction, of worldly enticement, of error's seduction, of sinful affections.

For Thine is the kingdom, etc. Thy kingdom governs all, Thy power subdues all, Thy glory is above all.

Amen. As it is in Thy purposes, so it is in Thy promises ; so be it in our prayers, so shall it be to Thy praise.

### Man

Gen. ii. 7.

1. The meanness of his material—the dust of the ground.

2. The greatness of his Maker—the Lord God.

3. The excellence of his life—He breathed into his nostrils.

4. The limit of his nature—Adam was made a living soul.

### Manna

*A Type of Christ.*

John vi. 32–35.

*Mysterious.* Its name was—What is it? Jesus was not understood (Isa. liii. 2).

*Small.* Jesus was humble (Phil. ii. 8).

*Round.* Emblem of His eternity, without beginning or end (Heb. vii. 3).
*White.* Representing His purity (Heb. vii. 26).
*Sweet.* Type of His grace (John i. 6).
*Heavenly.* It came from above.
The commonest article upon the table is the fullest type of Christ.

### Many Mansions

John xiv. 2.

1. Christ always speaks of invisible world with certainty and familiarity. He has dwelt in both. Family element, first relationships among mankind. Heaven is the Father's house.
2. Possess Church on earth. Church in heaven. Survey wonders of earthly house, and the stupendous glory of heavenly *mansions* in contrast to tent-lodging. *Great variety*, diversity. *Numerous*, numberless throng. *Purity*, repose, superlative blessedness. Happiness of heaven many sided.
3. *Preparation.* Before the foundation of the world. Final reunion of families. Great joy, great love, great reward.

### Meet for the Master's Use

2 Tim. ii. 21.

Christ's relationship to us. Saviour, Redeemer, Friend, Keeper, Leader, and Master.
Contemplates using us. Conditions of service, wholly, absolutely, and without reserve.
No reserves. Willing, even with uncongenial duties.
No glorification of self. Self-esteem versus lowliness of mind.
Must be clean vessels. Blessed are the pure, etc. May be but an earthen vessel, yet acceptable.
Made fit, even altered by furnace of affliction and trial. Suffering, or prosperity, or adversity, become apt scholars in God's school.

### Missionaries, The First

Acts xiii. 1–13.

Faithfulness in lesser work is preparation for a higher sphere (*v.* 1).
Missionary work demands the best men (*v.* 1).

Better be a fellow-sufferer with a saint than a fellow-persecutor with a tetrarch (*v.* 1).

Missionaries sent out by prayer will be likely to return in triumph (*v.* 3).

If not in the first rank be willing to assist (*v.* 5).

Those who know most are most anxious to learn (*v.* 7).

False prophets seek men's money, true teachers seek men's souls (*vv.* 6–8).

Error and selfishness have good reason to fear the truth (*v.* 9).

The theory which leaves out judgment may be pleasant, but it is *not true* (*vv.* 10, 11).

The punishment for shirking work is to be denied work (*v.* 13). (Acts xv. 38.)

### Murmuring, Ten Arguments against

It speaks out many a root of bitterness to be strong in thy soul.

Is a mother sin, that breeds many other sins in disobedience, contempt, ingratitude, impatience, distrust, rebellion.

Is a God-provoking sin.

Is the devil's image, sin, and punishment, as he is still murmuring at every mercy that God bestows.

Is a mercy embittering sin.

Unfits the soul for duty.

Unmans a man.

Is a time-destroying sin.

Makes the life of man invisibly miserable.

### Nathanael's Prejudice

John i. 48.

His efforts as a genuine truth-seeker—
  He hearkens to information concerning truth.
  He renounces a prejudice against truth.
  He prosecutes an inquiry in search of truth.
In this he is influenced by the words of Philip—
  He is greeted by Christ.   He is struck by conviction.
His success as a genuine truth-seeker—
  He found in Christ a Divine Teacher, a Divine King.
His reward.   He saw great things.   He would see greater—A new universe, a new class of intelligence, a new order of ministry, and a new centre of attraction.

### Nehemiah and his Work
### Neh. i.

The court of a heathen prince may be the sanctuary to a Christian (*v.* 1).

Great movements for good often originate with one person (*v.* 1).

What is in the heart will come to the lips (*v.* 2).

Prayer is a sure refuge in trial (*v.* 4).

The reproach of God's people should be ours (*v.* 4).

If God were not more mindful of His promises than we are of His precepts, we were undone (*vv.* 8, 9).

The best way to reach men is through God (*v.* 11).

Favour with men is compatible when it springs from the favour of God (*v.* 11).

### New Year's Resolutions
### Ps. xxvii.

A new start. Three thoughts about God.

Light. How to see.

Salvation. How to be safe.

Strength. How to be strong.

How to see. The year a path. 365 steps. Light within (John i. 9). Light without (Ps. cxix. 105).

How to be safe. Danger to life and limb (Ps. cxix. 117).

How to be strong. "A safe stronghold our God is still."—*Luther's Hymn.*

Love for God's House—
When? Constantly (*v.* 4).
Why? To see God's beauty or pleasantness.
To ask questions (Ps. lxxiii. 17).

Habit of prayer—
For all things (*vv.* 5, 6).
Mercy (*v.* 7).
A vision of God's face (*v.* 8).
Prayer for God's presence (*vv.* 9, 10).
Prayer for guidance (*v.* 11).
Prayer for deliverance (*v.* 12).
At all times. Stated times. Uprising and lying down.

### No. 1

One is God's number. Signifies unity. God is one (James ii. 19).

Bible begins with God (Gen. i. 1). Jesus said, "I am Alpha" (Rev. i. 8; xi. 17).

Only one window in Ark, "that above" (Gen. vi. 16).

Noah had to look up. One window to our lives, "Jesus only" (Matt. xvii. 8 ; Heb. xii. 2).

One door to tabernacle (Exod. xxix. 11). Jesus said, " I am the door " (John x. 7).

One brazen altar (Exod. xxvii. 1 ; 1 Pet. i. 18, 19).

One sacrifice that many might go free (John xviii. 8 ; Heb. ix. 26).

The unity of God requires the unity of His people. The children of Israel had but one camp, one laver, one ark, one mercy-seat, one cloud, one High Priest. We are one in Christ (Gal. iii. 28). One body in Christ (Rom. xii. 4, 5). We should be of one mind (Phil. i. 27).

### Old Age, A Happy

Ps. lxxi. 9.

Peculiar circumstances in old age renders the favour and presence of God necessary.

Old age is a time of little natural enjoyment. A time when the troubles of life not only increase, but become less tolerable.

Old age is a time that ought to command respect, and does so among dutiful children.

Old age is not a sin, but a crown of glory.

### Path of Life

Ps. xvi. 11.

A Guide. Thou.
A Traveller. Me.
A Way. The path.
The End. Life.

All solitary. One Guide. One traveller. One way. Only life. Bring all together and make them one.

### Paul at Rome

Acts xxviii. 20–31.

Man's obstacles are God's agents for good.

Public opinion is not a measure of right and wrong (*v.* 22).

Experience of the truth is the best preparation for its exposition (*v.* 23).

No remedy is so sure as the one that has been tested (*v.* 23).

When teacher and pupil are thoroughly in earnest no lesson seems long (*v.* 23).

Every sermon makes the sinner better or worse (*v.* 24).

Prejudice must be put away if we would accept the truth (*v.* 27).

As all roads lead to Rome, so all truth leads to Christ (*vv.* 23, 31).

### Paul's first Missionary Sermon

#### Acts xiii. 26–43.

Use the utmost courtesy in attracting men to the Gospel (*v.* 26).

The great message is not of wealth and honour, but salvation (*v.* 26).

The word sent, places men in a position of singular favour, notable indebtedness, great hopefulness, and serious responsibility.

It is a word of pardon for the sinner, life to the dead, liberty to the captive, direction to the bewildered, refreshment to the weary, comfort to the disconsolate, and strength to the weak.

Men may fulfil Scripture prophecy while breaking Scripture precepts (*v.* 27).

God will make man's wicked works glorify Him (*v.* 27).

Slaying Christ man did his worst (*v.* 28).

Resurrecting Christ God did His best (*v.* 30).

He who serves his generation serves all others (*v.* 36).

He who fails cannot serve any other (*v.* 36).

Our time for service here is limited (*v.* 36).

Knowledge is the root of responsibility (*v.* 38). (James iv. 17.)

### Paul's Shipwreck

#### Acts xxvii. 30–44.

Perils bring out our meannesses (*v.* 25), or our nobleness (*v.* 43).

God's way must be our way (*v.* 31).

Weak and trembling Christians need to feast on Christ for strength (*v.* 34).

Example is the most effective preaching (*v.* 35).

Good cheer can only come from a good man.

No promise of God is an excuse for lack of earnest effort (*v.* 40).

The wreck of temporal things may become the very means of our salvation (*v.* 44).

Happy they who reach heaven, though they lose all in the attempt (*v.* 44).

God fulfils all His promises to the letter (*v.* 44).

### Peace with God

Rom. v. 1.

I. In the affections.
II. In the will.
III. In the conscience.

We have peace with God, because the bad past is blotted out.

We have peace with God because, being justified, we are no longer condemned.

We have peace with God because our warfare against God ceases and friendship is begun.

We have peace with God because of His smile and approval.

### Peter and the Risen Lord

John xxi. 17.

The unknown Saviour on the shore.
A night of fruitless toil.
The great harvest of the morning.
Love discovers the Lord.
Zeal hastens to touch Him.
The gracious invitation, and awe-stricken disciples.
The thrice-repeated question and command.

### Peter's Deliverance from Prison

Acts xii. 1–17.

The ministry is a divine calling (*v.* 1).

Bad men care more to please men than God (*v.* 3).

Those who please men are an easy prey to Satan (*v.* 3).

The nearest way to all success is by the throne (*v.* 5).

God sets a limit to the wickedness of the wicked (*v.* 6).

There is no difficulty that God cannot meet (*v.* 7).

God holds all forces and all beings under His control (*v.* 7).

When the angel of the Lord comes to deliver, follow him (*v.* 9).

Extraordinary dealings continue no longer than necessary (*v.* 10).

If there be a knot you cannot untie, cut it with prayer (*v.* 12).

Marvel at the *way* God answers prayer, but never at the *fact* (*v.* 15).

That God gives marvellous deliverance is no reason why we should not use common prudence (*v.* 17).

### Philip and the Eunuch

#### Acts viii. 26.

God's will and direction often seem strange.

Man's purposes not untrue and accord with His.

Christians had assembled in Jerusalem. Outpouring of the Holy Ghost. Then dispersed over the known world. Thus was the Gospel seed sown. Soon opposition aroused. Stephen stoned. Philip succeeds to his office.

Receives a call to go ; no hesitancy ; leaves a great work to go to a congregation of one in the desert.

Learn to listen for God's call, then obey. Human nature prone to linger. Larger spheres of usefulness open up in a mysterious way. The Eunuch carried the good tidings to a far country. So we, as Christians, where we go should sow and spread the seed of the Gospel of the Kingdom.

### Prayer

#### John xvi. 23, 24.

Human life is the expression of a want ; its inner movement is desire for something unattained. Man's untiring demands must look ever upwards to the Father's face.

1. Human life is a life of asking and a life of prayer.

2. The name of Jesus is to put all man's askings to the proper proof. In My Name. "Feeble and stammering our lips may be, but the advocacy of Jesus is all powerful."

The name is redemptive in winning for us a favourable hearing.

### Prayer, Answers to

#### Ps. xii. 5.

God takes notice of every grace.

To *fear* His name is no great matter, yet these have a promise.

To *think* on His name less, yet set down in the book of remembrance.

A *desire* is a small matter, especially ot the poor man.

God regards the good desire as great kindness.

A *tear* makes no great noise, yet the voice of weeping is heard.

A *groan* is a poor thing, yet often it is the best part of a prayer.

A *sigh* is less, yet God is awakened by it.

The Lord aroused. How? Why? What to do? When?

### Prayer, Lesson on

Luke xviii. 9–17.

Men who know themselves never despise others (*v.* 9).

If we justify ourselves (*v.* 9) God condemns us (*v.* 14).

A prayer without penitence is a bird without wings (*v.* 11).

Go to the temple to pray, not to pass judgment (*v.* 11).

Give a tenth, and don't brag about it (*v.* 12).

Better reckon sins than recount virtues (*v.* 13).

You can see God as a Saviour when you see yourself a sinner (*v.* 14).

He who exalts himself is not worthy to be exalted (*v.* 17).

### Prayer, Instruction in

Luke xi. 9.

Ask—Boldly, Largely, Intelligently, Submissively, Specifically.

Seek—Diligently, Persistently, Assuredly, Personally, Humbly.

Knock—Patiently, Expectantly, Earnestly.

As
See
Knoc **K**

### Prayer, Prevailing

Gen. xxxii. 26.

Study Jacob's prayer, offered to God of his father, grounded on and crowned with a promise.

A confession : I am not worthy.

Humble : he not true to God, but God true to him.

Grateful (*v*. 10).

Definite : Deliver me from Esau (*v*. 11).

Prevailing prayer springs from a consciousness of need definitely stated.

Jacob's plan (*vv*. 13-23).

Jacob's power (*vv*. 24-30).

Place of solitude.  Place of defeat.  Place of desperation and confession.

### Prayer, Private

We grow, we wax mighty, we prevail.

To be strong to labour ⎫
Tender to sympathise ⎬ let us pray.
Wise to direct ⎭

If study makes men of us, prayer will make saints of us.

Sacred furnishing for a holy life, found only in the arsenal of supplication.

Consecrated warfare.

Prayer alone can keep our armour bright.

### Precious Things (Eight)

1. God's Thoughts (Ps. cxxxix. 17).
2. Corner Stone (Isa. xxviii. 16 ; 1 Pet. ii. 4, 6, 7).
3. Blood of Christ (1 Pet. i. 19).
4. Faith (2 Pet. i. 1).
5. Trial of Faith (1 Pet. i. 7).
6. Promises (2 Pet. i. 4).
7. Fruit Patience (Jas. v. 7).
8. Death of His saints (Ps. cxvi. 15).

### Prodigal Son

Luke xv.

#### IN TWO CHAPTERS

| *Chapter* i. | *Chapter* ii. |
|---|---|
| Rashness. | Repentance. |
| Revelling. | Resolution. |
| Reaping. | Return. |
| Remorse. | Reward. |
| Reflection. | Rejoicing. |

### Promise, A

Phil. iv. 19.

#### FAITH'S BANK NOTE.

*Name of Banker.*  My God.  The Infinite, Almighty, never-changing One.

*Promise to pay.* "Shall supply." A blind woman had certain promises in Bible marked with pins, and placing her fingers upon them, pleaded : "Here is Thine own word, Lord."

*Amount.* All you need.

*Bank Capital.* According to His riches (Eph. iii. 16 ; Ps. lxxxiv. 12).

*Location of the Bank.* In glory.

*Cashier.* With Him all things (Rom. viii. 32) ; without Him nothing (John xv. 5).

### Promises of God

2 Sam. vii. 4–16.

Apprehend them, by meditation, quietness, service, humility.

Accept them. He is able to perform, faithful to His word. Large (John xiv. 14).

Appreciate them. Acknowledge them.

Appropriate them. A promise is like a cheque. A prayer should be the presentation of God's promise endorsed by personal faith. Brings joy—of memory, of experience, of anticipation.

### Psalm, First, The

1. Three steps into outer darkness—neglecting, rejecting, despising. Those only truly happy that are truly holy.

2. What we delight in shows what we are. Whatever we need to be, to do, or to know, begins with meditation on the Word. Study of Bible not only a duty, but a delight.

3. Sin puts a negative on every blessing.

4. The sinner to be for ever separated from the saint.

5. Though the way of righteous may be clouded, yet the Lord knoweth it.

### Psalms, Book of

The key-word to the Psalms is Jesus the Messiah, and He the "object" and the "subject." "In the volume of the book it is written of *me*" (Ps. xl. 7).

Psalms are full of His humiliation, rejection, meditation, resurrection, intercession, exaltation, and final triumph.

The book begins with blessing and ends with praise. Hebrew title, "Praises." Greek title, "Songs set to music." The writers penned, under the inspiration of the Holy Spirit, songs of the Redeemer for the universal heart of the redeemed.

Ps. xviii., Deliverance psalm.

Ps. xxxii., Pardon psalm.

Ps. xlv., Marriage psalm. Key to Solomon's Song.

Ps. xlvi., Faith psalm. Begins and ends with refuge.

Ps. lxii., Confidence psalm.

Ps. lxxxviii., Saddest psalm.

Ps. xci., Safety psalm. Twenty-four promises.

Ps. ci., Householders' psalm.

Ps. cvii., Gratitude. Sailors' psalm.

Ps. cxviii., Lord spoken of forty-six times.

Ps. cxix., Christian A B C of the praise, love, power and use of the Word.

Ps. cxxi., Travellers' psalm.

Ps. cxxxii., three requests and three answers.

Ps. cxlv., All praise.

Ps. cxlvi–cl., Begin and end with Hallelujah.

### Psalms of David

The Greeks call the book the Soul's Anatomy, the Tongue of David, the Garden of Scripture, and the Rosary of Promises. Origen says the Holy Scriptures are locked with the key of David.

The twenty-third is the nightingale of the Psalms, of small homely feather, singing shyly out of obscurity; but it has filled the world with melody, singing in every language, and charming more griefs to rest than all the philosophy of the world.

The forty-sixth is called Luther's psalm. When in trouble he would say, " Let us sing the forty-sixth psalm." His great choral has voiced the faith and joy of God's people for centuries.

Ps. cxix., the Saints' Alphabet. Matthew Henry says that it is rather a chest of gold rings than of gold links, having an ingenious artificial form instead of logical order.

### Question, An Important

" *Do ye now believe ?* "—John xvi. 31.

Questions abound in this gospel—ten in the first chapter. Christ often subjected to examination and cross-examination. Sometimes He becomes the questioner.

A plain question. Characteristics of the gospel message and appeal.

A practical question. Concerns daily life.

A personal question. God deals with men as individuals and as congregations.

A pressing question, now.

Must be answered.

### Quit you like men
#### 1 Cor. xvi. 13.

The man who is always talking war is a coward. The true warrior is the man who loves peace, but when war is forced upon him fights like seven men. The men who move the world are the men whom the world can't move.

Essential to Christian growth and development :—

A pure atmosphere (Phil. iv. 8).

A good appetite (Matt. v. 6).

Best food—bread (John vi. 51).

Milk (1 Pet. ii. 2).

Meat (1 Cor. iii. 2).

Sunshine (Mal. iv. 2).

Light (2 Cor. iv. 6).

Exercise, light (Eph. v. 2, 8).

Exercise, gradual (1 Cor. ix. 24).

Rest (Mark vi. 31).

### Raising of Lazarus
#### John xi. 30-45.

Where there are mourners there ought to be comforters (v. 31).

Thinking what might have been only adds to our sorrow (v. 32).

No affliction would trouble us if we knew God's reasons for it (v. 32).

Sympathy is Christlike (v. 35).

If you admit Christ to your home, He will come to you at the grave (v. 38).

Do whatever God bids you without objecting (v. 39).

Human service may prepare the way for Divine power (v. 39).

Unbelief ignores miracles because of difficulties (v. 39).

Faith ignores difficulties because of miracles (v. 40).

A time of affliction is a time for faith (v. 40).

As God answers before we call, we should praise before He grants (v. 41).

### Remembrance

Ps. lxxvii. 6.

A good memory is helpful and useful.

A means of knowledge. A means of faith (1 Cor. xv. 2).

A means of comfort and thankfulness. A means of hope (Rom. v. 4).

Experience worketh hope, and memory is the storehouse of experience.

A means of repentance. How can we mourn over what we have forgotten?

A means of usefulness. A spark of grace kindled spreads soon.

### Resurrection, Facts of the

1 Cor. xv. 13, 14.

*Primal* fact. Great, supernatural, all-important, fundamental.

*Prominent* fact. Christ died.

Predicted fact. According to the Scriptures.

*Proved* fact. Risen Christ now seen of Cephas, of twelve, of 500, of James.

Prefigured fact.

Powerful fact. By the grace of God I am what I am (*v.* 10).

Proclaimed fact. *So* we preached (*vv.* 13, 14).

Pronounced fact. Now *is* Christ risen (*v.* 20). Echoed through the ages.

### Resurrection of Christ

Luke xxiv. 1-12.

God works where love leads (*v.* 2).

The way of humiliation is the way of triumph (*v.* 3).

Unbelief will be "perplexed" at the greatest blessings (*v.* 4).

We cannot find Christ in ceremony, law, reform, or philosophy (*v.* 5).

Life, not death, is our companion (*v.* 5; John xiv. 6).

If we remember our Lord's words, we shall understand His providences (*v.* 8).

Great truths are not always accepted at once (*v.* 11).

Earth is slow to believe Heaven's message (*v.* 11).

Give God's Word and wait; some will run and wonder and believe (*v.* 12).

### Resurrection of Christ

Matt. xxviii. 1–10.

Seek God early (*v.* 1 ; Matt. vi. 33).

Let every morning remind us of Christ's resurrection and coming (*v.* 1).

If help from earth fails us, God will send it from heaven (*v.* 3).

"Come," and get salvation ; then go and proclaim it (*vv.* 6, 7).

Christ wants practical, active servants (*v.* 8).

To hearts of love and hands of service Christ is first revealed (*v.* 9).

No man can go on God's errands without His company (*v.* 9).

The world may boast of its titles. We who are called His " brethren " have the highest (*v.* 10).

### Revival of Religion

Ps. xiv. 7.

I. Frequent condition of the Church—captivity.

II. Means of revival—the Lord's coming in grace.

III. Consequences—"rejoice," "be glad."

Captivity of the soul. What it is. How provided for. How accomplished. With what results.

### Righteous, Character of

Ps. v. 11.

Faith and love.

Privileges of the righteous.

1. Joy, great, pure, satisfying, triumphant, constant ever.

Joy in the Lord both a duty and privilege.

2. Defence, by power, providence, angels, grace, etc.

### Rock, God our

Salvation (2 Sam. xxii. 47).

Stability (Matt. vii. 24, 25 ; xvi. 18).

Security (Ps. xciv. 22).

Shelter (Ps. lxi. 3).

Satisfaction (1 Cor. x. 4).

Strength (Ps. xxxi. 2).

Shadow (Isa. xxxii. 2).

### Romans, Epistle to the, Features, etc., of

In it there are sixty-one quotations from the Old Testament.

The name of God is prominent in the epistle, occurring twenty-two times in first chapter.

A catechism for Christians, and a perfect body of apostolic doctrine.  The most profound book in existence.

Chrysostom would have it read to him twice a *week*.

Luther says it is the masterpiece of the New Testament, the gospel in its perfect purity.

### Salvation, God's Purpose in our

God-ward (Deut. v. 5).
Christ-ward (1 Cor. i. 9).
Spirit-ward (1 Cor. vi. 19).
Saint-ward (John xiii. 34, 35).
World-ward (John xvii. 16).
Satan-ward (1 John ii. 14).
Self-ward (Luke ix. 23).

### Saul's Conversion

#### Acts ix.

A false religion is bloodthirsty (*v.* 2).

Mighty hate (*v.* 1) can be conquered by mighty love (*v.* 4).

Humble conviction is the first step towards saving conversion (*v.* 4).

A sight of Jesus will convict and convert (*v.* 5).

While the bodily eyes are shut the spiritual may be open (*v.* 9).

A devout disciple will be a Divine messenger (*v.* 11).

Every Christian's work is allotted to him by God (*v.* 15).

To be honoured with much service involves the honour of much suffering (*v.* 16).

Two great needs of every convert—more light and the abiding power of the Spirit (*v.* 17).

### Saving Faith

#### Heb. x. 39.

Apostle exhorts the Hebrews to constancy in Christian faith and obedience.

*Faith, its nature.*  It is belief in another's testimony.  Belief in God's testimony concerning the Redeemer.  Trust in Christ as our Saviour.

*Faith, its origin.*  It is of God.  He produces faith by the Holy Spirit.

The *instrument*, or means by which faith is produced and maintained.  By hearing, and hearing by

the Word of God. Fellowship with God enriches.
Men of prayer are men of faith. Closet supplications
make faith's heroes.

*Degrees of faith.* Effects and evidences of faith.
It imparts peace, produces holiness, purifies the heart,
overcomes the world, prepares for heaven.

### Scripture Emblems

1. Lamp, lantern, light (Ps. cxix. 105; Prov. vi. 23).
2. Fire (Jer. xxiii. 29).
3. Hammer (Jer. xxiii. 29).
4. Sharp sword (Eph. vi. 17; Heb. iv. 12).
5. Graft (Jas. i. 21).
6. Glass mirror (Jas. i. 23, 24).
7. Pure milk (1 Pet. ii. 2).
8. Food of the soul (Jer. xv. 16).

### Scriptures, Search the

John v. 39.

S ystematically (Luke xxiv. 27; 2 Tim. ii. 14).
C arefully (Ps. i. 2).
R everently (Ps. xix. 7–11).
I ntently (Prov. ii. 2). Why? (Heb. v. 12.)
P rayerfully (Jas. i. 5–7; Ps. cxix. 18).
T rustingly (John xx. 31; Acts xxiv. 14).
U nderstandingly (Acts viii. 30). Why? (Heb. iv.
    12.)
R etentively (Jer. xx. 9; Ps. cxix. 11).
E very day (Acts xvii. 11; 1 Pet. ii. 2).
S avingly (Acts xx. 32).

### Season of Grace

2 Cor. vii. 10.

Sin, repentance and pardon are like to the three
vernal months of the year—March, April, and May.

*Sin* comes in like March, blustering, stormy, and
full of bold violence.

*Repentance* succeeds like April—showery, weeping,
and full of tears.

*Pardon* follows like May—springing, singing, full
of joys and flowers.

Our *eyes* must be full of April with the sorrow of
repentance.

Then our *hearts* shall be full of May with the true
joy of forgiveness.

### Seed Thoughts for Spiritual Farming

Seed to use (Luke viii. 11).
Seed to avoid (Joel i. 17).
When to sow (Eccles. xi. 6).
Spring medicine (Ezek. xlvii. 12).
Shoes for feet (Eph. vi. 15).
Insure the crops (Rom. viii. 28).
Summer morning prayer (Ps. xvi. 1).
Summer evening prayer (Ps. iv. 8).
Sure harvest (Ps. cxxvi. 6).

### Seek

*What* shall we seek?
Seek ye first the kingdom (Matt. vi. 33).
Seek those things which are above (Col. iii. 1).
Seek peace and pursue it (Ps. xxxiv. 14).
*Where* should we seek?
Seek ye out of the book (Isa. xxxiv. 16),
Seek the law at his mouth (Mal. ii. 7).
*When* should we seek?
Seek me early (Prov. viii. 17).
Early will I seek (Ps. lxiii. 1).
Seek ye first the kingdom (Matt. vi. 33).
*Whom* should we seek?
Seek ye the Lord (Isa. lv. 6).
Seek the Lord (Amos v. 6).
*What* promises to those that seek?
Seek, and ye shall find (Luke xi. 19).
Success—the Lord is good (Lam. iii. 25).
Satisfaction—All these things shall be added (Luke xii. 31).
*How* should we seek?
Seek by prayer (Dan. ix. 13).
Diligently (Prov. xi. 27).
Intensely (Jer. xxix. 13).
With all your heart.

### Self-Control (Sermon for Young Men)

"*And when forty years were expired,*" etc.
Acts vii. 30 and 35.

Greenhouse plants lovely but not strong.
The oak tree strong and hardy, able to stand the cold wintry wind, etc.
Hearts of oak have all true men.
Moses chosen by God for a grand work.

He had to learn the lesson of self-restraint.

An engine must have plenty of steam power, but it must be properly controlled.

Man's passions are like that steam power.

Christ was seized with a passionate longing to teach the Scribes and Pharisees, but restrained Himself till He was thirty years.

Self-denial, restraint, hardships—the school to which God sends all His heroes.

Self-knowledge, self-control, self-reverence, God alone can form in us.

### Selling the Birthright

Gen. xxv. 27-34.

Favouritism injures the favoured, the unfavoured, and him who shows it (*v*. 28).

Those that work are better provided for than those that hunt (*v*. 29).

Trifles are the truest test of character (*v*. 30).

We cannot help ourselves to Canaan by mean things (*v*. 31).

A good motive does not justify unworthy means (*v*. 31).

Never choose present gratification before future good (*v*. 32).

Learn to be strong to resist.

Learn to be generous to give.

Learn to be determined never to deceive.

Learn to be above taking advantage.

### Service of God, For the

Ezra vi. 20.

True service begins with a recognition of God's ownership.

To be dedicated is to be separated (*vv*. 19, 21).

Socially, Marital—not unequally yoked. Commercial (1 Cor. x. 31).

Political (Matt. iv. 9). Citizenship (Phil. iii. 20).

Ecclesiastical (Jude 20, 23).

### Set Apart

Ps. iv. 3.

Godly are precious, therefore set apart.

We set apart precious things, and so God acts.

As His peculiar treasure (Ps. cxxxv. 4).

As His garden of delight (Cant. iv. 12).
As His royal diadem (Isa. xliii. 3).
The godly are the excellent of the earth (Ps. xvi. 3).
Comparable to fine gold (Lam. iv. 2).
Doubly refined (Zech. xiii. 9).
Glory of His Creation (Isa. xlvi. 13).
Jewels (Mal. iii. 17).

### Seven Baptisms of Scripture

1. Baptism of Deluge.   Death of old world.
Resurrection of new (Gen. vii. 21 ; 1 Pet. iii. 20).
2. Baptism of Red Sea.   Death to Egypt (Exod.
xiv. 22 ; 1 Cor. x. 2).
3. Baptism of Jordan.   Death to wilderness
wanderings (Josh. iv. 10).
4. Baptism of John.   Death to Judaism unto
repentance (Matt. iii. 1, 5, 6, 11).
5. Christian Baptism.   Following the Lord in
death and resurrection (Rom. vi. 3, 4).
6. Baptism of Holy Spirit.   Into one body (1 Cor.
xii. 13 ; Acts ii. 4).
7. Baptism of Fire (Matt. iii. 11 ; Heb. xii. 29).

### Seven Chosen Things

Abraham, in whom all nations are blessed (Gen.
xviii. 18).
Israel, as a peculiar and separated people (Deut.
vii. 6).
Moses, as deliverer of God's people (Exod. iii. 10).
Christ, as Saviour of the world (John iv. 42).
Disciples, to be witnesses of the truth (John xv. 16).
Paul, to be the apostle to the Gentiles (Acts ix. 15).
Us, the weak and ignorant, to be His children
(1 Cor. i. 27 ; Matt. xx. 16).

### Sevens of the Bible

Steps (Phil. ii. 6, 7, 8).
Things the Lord hates (Prov. vi. 16-19).
Musts of the Bible (Acts xvi. 30 ; John iii. 7 ;
John iii. 14 ; Acts iv. 12 ; Ezra x. 12 ; Luke xix. 5 ;
2 Cor. v. 10).

### Seven, Number

Rainbow, seven colours.
Lord's prayer, seven petitions.
Seven words in sinner's prayer.   Three God-ward,
four man-ward (Luke xviii. 13).

E

Seven promises (Gen. xii. 2, 3).
Seven things God is to us (Ps. xviii. 2).
Seven things Christ became for us (Phil. ii. 5, 8).
Seven praises (Rev. v. 12).
Seven commands (1 Thess. v. 16–21).
Seven pronouns (John xvi. 13).
Seven-fold covenant (Exod. vi. 6–8).

### Seven Links in the Chain

Crucified together with Christ (Gal. ii. 20).
Quickened together with Christ (Col. ii. 13).
Raised together with Christ (Eph. ii. 5).
Seated together with Christ (Eph. ii. 7).
Sufferers together with Christ (Rom. viii. 17)
Heirs together with Christ (Rom. viii. 17).
Glorified together with Christ (Rom. viii. 17).
The first and second are seen at the cross and grave
of Christ.
The third to sixth form our present privilege.
The seventh has its scene in the future.

### Seven Promises for Seven Needs

Tired (Isa. xl. 29, 31).
Hungry (Isa. xl. 11).
Thirsty (Isa. xli. 18).
Fearful (Isa. xli. 10, 13).
Troubled (Isa. xxvi. 34).
Tempted (Isa. lix. 19).
Fighting (Isa. liv. 17).
Whatsoever state thou art (Isa. xlix. 16).

### Seven Rules for Spiritual Living

Look diligently (Heb. xi. 15).
Wait patiently (Ps. xl. 1).
Stand continually (Isa. xxi. 8).
Walk humbly (Micah vi. 8).
Run well (Gal. v. 7).
Provide honestly (Rom. xii. 17).
Lie down trustingly (Rom. xii. 18).

### Seven Things Opened

Eyes (Isa. xlii. 7).
Ears (Isa. l. 5).
Heart (Acts xvi. 14).

Mouth (Ps. li. 15).
Scriptures (Luke xxiv. 32).
Understanding (Luke xxiv. 45).
Door for service (1 Cor. xvi. 9).

### Seven Things Christians should do

They should live—
1. A life of holiness (1 Thess. v. 22 ; 2 Tim. ii. 19).
2. A life of prayer (1 Tim. ii. 8 ; 1 Thess. v. 17).
3. A life of death (Heb. xi. 6 ; Col. i. 23).
4. A life of self-denial (Matt. v. 29 ; Gal. v. 24).
5. A life of separation from world (Exod. xxxii. 26).
6. A life of consecration (Exod. xxviii. 40, 41 ; Rom. xii. 1).
7. A life of service (Deut. x. 12 ; Luke xvi. 13).

### Silence, A Seven-fold
Ps. xxxix. 2.

Stoical, politic, foolish, sullen, forced, despairing, prudent, holy and gracious silence.

### Sin and its Punishments
Ps. li.

Sin, and what it does—
It defiles us (*vv*. 2, 7).
Haunts us (*v*. 3).
Makes us sad (*v*. 8).
Brings condemnation (*v*. 9).
Drives us from God's presence (*v*. 11).
    Adam hid (Gen. iii. 8).    Cain fled (Gen. iv. 16).
    Judas hanged himself (Matt. xxvii. 5).
Grieves the Holy Spirit (*v*. 11).
Robs of joy (*v*. 12).
Destroys our testimony (*vv*. 13, 15).
Puts a stumbling-block in the way of others (*v*. 14).
Closes our lips (*v*. 15).
Brings punishment (2 Sam. xii. 15-23).

### Sin, Foolishness of
Ps. xxxviii. 5.

The folly of sin. Everything that a man has to do with sin shows his folly.
    Dallying with sin.
    Committing it.
    Continuing in it.
    Hiding it.
    Palliating it.

### Sin and Justification

Rom. iii. 19-26.

Sin closes our lips, grace opens them (*v.* 19).

Gospel excludes none that do not exclude themselves (*v.* 22).

Faith in Christ is not a condition of merit but of mercy (*v.* 24).

Blessings from Christ's death reach backward as well as forward (*v.* 25).

Justification is offered on easy terms ; only so could man receive it (*v.* 26).

### Sleep, A Pillow for

To sleep well, lay these under your head as pillow :—

1. A precious promise out of the Scriptures.
2. A sweet verse of some evangelical hymn.
3. A hearty prayer to God.
4. A good conscience purified with Christ's blood.
5. A feeling of forgiveness and charity to all mankind.
6. A resolution to serve God better on the morrow.
7. A glance of faith at the Cross.

### Slippery Places

1 Cor. x. 12.

Four places to warn against—
  Self-confidence.
  Ignorance of weak points in one's character.
  Curiosity to see life.
  Financial successes.
Venture not too near slippery places.
If duty requires, then watch.

### Slowness of Heart

Luke xxiv. 25.

Slow brains, dense and dull of perception.
Slow men, lazy, indolent.
Slow preachers.    Put a fullstop at every word.
Slow of heart faith, slow to believe.
Slow of heart loyalty.    Loyalty appears when trouble comes.
  Slow of heart perception.    To recognise Christ.
  Slow of heart testimony.    Not willing to testify.

## Solomon's Wise Choice
### I Kings iii. 5-15.

1. If the day has been busy for Him the night will be easy in Him (*v.* 5).
2. Dreams show character (*v.* 5).
3. The memory of a holy life is a blessed legacy (*v.* 6).
4. To feel one's ignorance is a step to wisdom (*v.* 7).
5. He will try to learn who finds how little he knows (*v.* 7).
6. Prefer grace to gold (*v.* 9).
7. What we ask tests our character and determines our destiny (*v.* 10).
8. Prayer is taking hold of God's willingness (*v.* 11).
9. Higher good brings with it all lesser blessings (*vv.* 13, 14).

## Sowing and Reaping
### Gal. vi. 7.

God will use us as an example or as warnings. We decide which.

A bad man is never so bad as when pretending to be a saint.

There is an inspiration of the devil as well as that of the Spirit.

A wicked thought entertained is a door opened to Satan.

Sometimes the greatest severity is the greatest mercy.

Sad to see relatives that should help one another to good, harden one another to evil.

Concealed sin, as well as public iniquity, will be judged.

## Spiritual Harvesting
### John iv. 35, 36.

As much encouragement to attempt to bless souls as farmer to seek a crop, and to expect revivals of religion, as harvest follows seed time.

*The work.* Spiritual results. To gather a soul. Value the worth of a soul. Harvest is promiscuous. Seek all. Souls, and not sects. Work divine, but gathered by human labourers.

*The worker.* Reaper must work hard. Harvest time is a busy time. Early and late. Reaper must go in among the grain, bring his sickle and use it.

Results of working. Wages, fruit, joy.

### Spirit of Truth

John xvi. 13.

Holy Spirit given for reproof and conviction of the world, also given for the enlightenment and edification of the Church.

I. Designation of Holy Spirit. The Father is the absolute Truth, one eternal source of truth. The Divine Son reveals, embodies, and bears witness to the truth.

The Holy Ghost coming into contact with souls brings truth home with power.

II. His coming. Full gift of Spirit when the full truth had been revealed in Christ.

III. His office. *Generally* — to lead Christians not into every kind of truth but the truth as in Jesus. *Specially*—to reveal what Christ is to His people. Help Christians to realize and appropriate blessings brought by Christ to man. *Prophetically*—to unfold things to come.

IV. His end and aim. The glory of Christ.

### Spiritual Remedies for Spiritual Maladies

Bad temper (Ps. xxxiv. 1).
Evil speaking (Ps. xxxv. 28).
Melancholy (Ps. lxx. 4).
Scandal (Ps. lxxi. 8).
Self-righteousness (Ps. lxxi. 15).
Fear (Ps. lxxi. 24).
Boasting (Ps. xliv. 8).
Envy (Prov. xxiii. 17).
Evil thoughts (Ps. cxix. 97).

### Stephen

*The first Christian Martyr.*

Acts vii. 54–60.

Enmity to God is heart cutting, in faith God is heart healing (*v.* 54).

Only Stephen's virtues can entitle us to Stephen's consolations (*v.* 55).

Heaven accepts what earth rejects (*v.* 55).
Heaven, though unseen, is not far away (*v.* 55).
Our brightest visions may come in our bitterest
trials (*v.* 56).
Raised to glory, the Son of man is never forgetful
of our sorrow (*v.* 56).
The blood of the martyrs is the seed of the Church
(Acts viii. *v.* 1).
Present loss may be abiding gain (*v.* 1).
God transforms hindrances into helps (*v.* 4).
Christians should preach the Word everywhere
(*v.* 4).

### Swear Not At All

#### Matt. v. 34.

It is mean to swear.   Dishonours God.
It is rude to swear.   Lack of good breeding.
Swearing is the sign of an empty head.   Senseless
and meaningless habit.
Swearing is wicked.   Breaking God's command.
Futile in its effort and effect.

### Teacher and the Taught (Christ and Nicodemus)

#### John iii. 1, 2.

1. *The Disciple.*   His relation to the ruling powers,
and his position as a man of culture.   His want of
moral courage.   His reverent acknowledgment of
Christ's authority.   His willingness to be taught.
2. *The Teacher.*   His willingness to teach.   Christ
ever meets the reverent inquirer in this spirit.   His
willingness to accept imperfect faith.
3. *The truths He taught.*   The need of regenera-
tion.   The mystery of His own person.   The great
purpose of His mission with the method of its accom-
plishment.

### Things to Hold Fast

That which is good (1 Thess. v. 21).
Faithful word (Titus i. 9).
Form of sound words (2 Tim. i. 13).
Confidence and rejoicing of hope (Heb. iii. 6).
Profession of our faith (Heb. x. 23).
That we have (Rev. iii. 11).
The unfaithful hold fast and repent (Rev. iii. 3).

### Three Young Men Tested

Dan. iii. 13-23 and Isa. xliii. 2.

Note some tests of Christianity (Dan. iii. 13-15).

I. Circumstances, authority, danger.

II. Be careful for nothing.

III. When tested prefer suffering to sin (Dan. iii. 17-23).

IV. See the limits of human power (*vv.* 19-25).

V. Know the blessing of the furnace.

Freedom, occupation, protection, companionship, deliverance, glory.


### Try or Trust

Try is of doubtful quantity, it implies incompleteness, dissatisfaction, discouragement.

Trust is confidential, restful, assured.

Try is cumbered with duties, observances, tasks attempted and never done.

Trust rises into an atmosphere of faith, hope, and love ; good works follow.

Try is restless, feverish, moved or arrested by moods and feelings.

Trust is peaceful, getting out of self to God.

Therefore, " Trust ye in the Lord for ever."


### Universal Creatorship of Christ

John i. 3.

1. Associates Christ's name with all existence, past and present. Furnishes the key to the dark problems of providence and nature. Gives science and Christianity a common foundation. Science reveals the eternal power and Godhead of the word. Christianity the means of mercy to the fallen world.

2. Affords to faith the greatest assurance and encouragement.

3. Inspires the humblest with confidence.

4. Irradiates the future with a glorious hope (Rev. xxi. 1-5). Christ's relation to the created universe. *In* Him. *By* Him. *For* Him.

### Vacant Places
I Sam. xx. 25.

Life reveals many vacancies.
In the family, leave sorrow in heart.
Vacant places here should mean occupied places in heaven.
In the social circle. Old friends gone.
Consolation in memory of those good.
In the house of God. Often from carelessness, indifference, whims, and fancies. Office-bearers, deacons, etc., soldiers in the Church's army roll-call, many not answer.
Left Church on earth to Church in heaven.
Memories of dead, deep and tender pathos.
Example left behind.
May we leave them, shortness of time, preparation.
Father's house above.

### W's Seven

Wash (Acts xxii. 16; Rev. vii. 14).
Walk (Rom. vi. 4).
Worship (Phil. iii. 3).
Work (Col. i. 10).
War (I Tim. i. 18, 19).
Watch (I Cor. xvi. 13).
Wait (I Thess. i. 10; 2 Thess. iii. 5).

### Waiting for the Lord
Ps. xxxiii. 20.

Includes 1. *Conviction.* A persuasion that the Lord is the supreme good.
2. *Desire.* Expressed by hungering and thirsting after righteousness.
3. *Hope.* The Christian's hourly position.
4. *Patience.* God is never slack concerning His promise.

### Waiting upon God
Ps. liii. 4.

*What* is it to call upon God ?

1. A drawing near to Him.
2. A speaking to Him (I Sam. i. 12, 13).
3. A praying to Him.

*How* should we call upon God ?

1. Reverently. God's holiness and our sinfulness.
2. Understandingly (1 Cor. xiv. 15).
3. Submissively and constantly.
4. Believingly and sincerely.

*How* it appears to be a sin not to call ?

1. He hath commanded it (Isa. lv. 6).
2. Praying one of the principal parts of worship.

*Who* are guilty of this sin ?

1. All who pray to any one else.
2. All who neglect either public, private, or
   family worship.
3. All who pray, but not aright.

### He giveth more Grace (Watchnight Thoughts)

#### Jas. iv. 6.

Grace. A sweet word. Anglo-Saxon word.
Plain.

Old year. 365 days of grace.

We need grace spiritual. More grace this New
Year.

We have proved the grace of God. Not exhausted.
A new supply, a second supply, a greater supply,
and an eternal supply.

Giveth. Free. Unstinted.

Seek it daily, always. He rewards those who
seek.

### Water of Life

#### John iv. 14.

The Saviour as ready to preach to an audience of
one as of a thousand. His usual plan to make
natural circumstances and common occurrences the
vehicles of divine truth. Here water is used as a
type of grace.

1. *In its Origin.* " The water that I shall give
Him." " By the grace of God I am what I am."
The stream of grace which follows us in our wilderness life flows from the smitten Rock. "That Rock
is Christ."

"Grace is flowing like a river."

Christ still stands crying, as on " the great day of

the feast," "If any man thirst, let him come unto Me and drink." But,

"We cannot think a gracious thought," etc.

2. *In its Character.* (*a*) Water cleanses. "Wash me and I shall be whiter than snow."

(*b*) Water satisfies. "Whosoever drinketh . . . shall never thirst."

(*c*) Water fertilises. "He shall be like a tree planted by the rivers of water, that bringeth forth his fruit in due season."

3. *In its Influence.* (*a*) Inward and secret. "In Him"—to enlighten, to lead, to bear witness of acceptance, to keep in peace.

(*b*) Abundant. "A well of water springing up." "Rivers of living water." "He giveth not the Spirit by measure."

(*c*) Eternal. "Unto everlasting life."

"The men of grace have found
Glory begun below."

## Wisdom's Warning
### Prov. i. 20-33.

God desires to be heard and heeded (*v.* 20).

He who would save men must go where they are (*v.* 21).

At last Divine retribution will go as far as human perversity (*v.* 25).

A bitter cry is the one that comes too late (*v.* 26).

Our destiny is determined by our fate (*v.* 31).

A tree not only lies as it falls, but falls as it leans (*v.* 31).

The prosperity which forgets God is the greatest calamity (*v.* 32).

A sense of safety brings peace (*v.* 33).

## Wonder, a Triple
### Ps. lxxi. 7.

1. Reference to *David*, to Christ and the Christian. David. Wonder as a man, king, and servant of God.

2. Reference to *Christ.* A wonder in His person, His life, His miracles, His teachings, His sufferings, and ascension and mediation.

3. Reference to a *Christian.* A wonder to himself, the world, to the wicked, and the angels in heaven.

### Wonderful Deliverance, A

*The three Hebrew children.*—Dan. iii. 13.

No man can be true to God, and not at some time unpopular (*v.* 13).
Faith is fearless (*v.* 16).
To worry is to sin (*v.* 16).
Only those who serve God can claim His protection and promises (*v.* 17).
God always delivers *from* death or *in* death (*v.* 17).
Rather suffer than sin (*v.* 18).
Whatever the issue, we must obey God (*v.* 18).
Danger is no excuse for wrong-doing (*v.* 19).
Those who live godly in Christ shall suffer.(*v.* 20).
Who falls for love of God shall rise again (*v.* 20).
If God walks with us in the furnace we lose nothing but earthly bonds (*v.* 25).
Christ's presence is the brightest joy of earth.

### Work for Christ

Commission (2 Cor. v. 20).
Messenger (Rev. xxii. 17).
Conditions (John xxi. 15, 17).
Motive (2 Cor. v. 14).
Field (Matt. xxv. 40).
Responsibility (Heb. xiii. 17 ; Matt. xxv. 28).
Strength (2 Cor. iii. 5 ; Phil. iv. 13).
Our instrument (2 Tim. ii. 15).
Success (Ps. cxxvi. 6).

### World's Need of Christians

John xvii. 15.

1. Because the world needs them.  Their example, lights of the world.  In their character, duties, and sufferings, show the influence of religion.  Godly men should be living epistles.  Testimony.  God's witnesses.  Their prayers.  The prayers of the Church are like Moses' rod.  Israel needed Elijah's prayers.  Jerusalem sinners needed the prayers that preceded the pentecostal visitation.  Sympathies.
2. Because they need the world.  Trial of their faith.
To prove the sincerity of their love.
For their progressive sanctification.

### Year, End of the

Remember the promises made at the beginning of
the year. How many been kept and how many
broken. The undone duties, how many and how
great. The page was so white and clean, is blotted
with sin. See record.

Unkept promises.
Neglected opportunities.
Slighted privileges.
Advantages spurned.
Vows unpaid.
Energies misdirected.
Dangerous delays.

### Zacchæus, Call of

Luke xix. 5.

Gracious, personal, urgent, humbling, royal, neces-
sary, abiding, sympathetic and successful call.
Led to *obedience*. Made haste. Obedience linked
with fellowship. *Faith*. Received Him.
*Confession* (v. 8). Generosity. Genuine pity will
produce generous conduct.
*Restitution*, half of goods.
An assuring call (v. 9).
A family call. At thine house.

### Zacchæus, Call of

Luke xix. 1–10.

Chief sinners often make chief saints (v. 2).
Riches and honours count nothing beyond the grave
(v. 3).
Natural man too short to see the glory of God (v. 4).
Jesus meets and satisfies every enquiring soul (v. 5).
Curiosity took Zacchæus up, but love drew him
down (v. 6).
Grace to the fallen still an offence to the self-
righteous (v. 7).
Conviction and condemnation followed by confession
and conversion (v. 8).
Jesus does it all, comes, seeks, and saves (v. 10).
The gospel of Jesus Christ not only delivers from
sin but self, not only Christ *for* me but Christ *in* me
(v. 10).

## THINGS WORTH THINKING ABOUT

### Bible, How to use the

As a lamp to guide (Ps. cxix. 105).
As a sword to defeat the devil (Eph. vi. 17).
As a hammer (Jer. xxiii. 29).
As food (Jer. xv. 16).
To comfort others (1 Thess. iv. 18).

### Bible, Study of the

*Topically.* Search out subjects such as Grace, Faith, Assurance, Hope, Heaven.
" Verilys " of John, " overcomes " of Revelation.
" Lookings " and " looking backs." " Beholds."
" I wills " in Psalms.    " I wills " of Christ.
*Books* essential—" Cruden's Concordance," and "Scripture Text-Book " (not Birthday), 1s. 6d. A.P.C.K., Dublin.
S earch (John v. 39 ; John ii. 12, 13).
E arnestly (Josh. i. 8 ; Ps. cxix. 12).
A nxiously (John xx. 31 ; Ps. cxix. 9).
R egularly (Acts xvii. 11 ; Ps. i. 2).
C arefully (Luke xxiv. 27 ; 2 Tim. iii. 16, 17).
H umbly (Luke xxiv. 45 ; Jas. i. 22).

### How to Prepare a Lesson or Sermon

1. Call to God for it (Ps. cxix. 18).
2. Choose a text (Luke iv. 17, 22).
3. Chew it (Josh. i. 8).
4. Compare it (Acts xvii. 11).
5. Commit it to memory (Deut. xi. 18).
6. Christ the centre (Luke xxiv. 27).
7. Continue to pray over it (Rom. xii. 12, R.V.).
8. Collect illustrations for it (Matt. xiii. 34).
9. Compare it with other sermons (1 Cor. ii. 13).
10. Condense it (Prov. x. 19).
11. Consecrate it (Ps. xxxvii. 5).

### Preaching, Essentials of

A definite theory.
Thoroughness of doctrinal knowledge.
Passion of living convictions.
Adaptation in statement.
Freedom in delivery.
A profound sense of dependence on the Holy Ghost.

### Preach the Truth

It is life (Phil. ii. 16).
It is light (Ps. cxix. 105).
It is power (Rom. i. 16).
It is pure (Ps. cxix. 140).
It is unchanging (Ps. cxix. 89).
It searches (Heb. iv. 12).
It judges (John xii. 48).

### How to make a Sermon

**Preparation.** Wilberforce said, some men prepare their sermons, some men prepare themselves. After self preparation comes intellectual preparation. Expository sermons need much careful treatment. Profit, not please the audience.

Louis XIV. comparing Massillon with the other Court preachers, remarked, leaving the chapel after hearing the other preachers: "I am pleased with myself"; leaving it after hearing Massillon, "I feel ashamed of myself."

It was said of Bishop Andrewes, those who stole his sermons could not steal his delivery. Mastery of subject would help to subdue self-consciousness. Divisions should be used, and stuck to. "Mouthing" was as detestable as "intoning." Speak naturally, distinctly, and from the heart.

## SUNDAY SCHOOL

### ESSENTIAL HINTS AND SUGGESTIONS

#### Sunday School Organization

Orderly arrangements (1 Cor. xiv. 40, 33).
Officers (1 Cor. xii. 28; 1 Kings iv. 1–7).
Financial (Neh. x. 32; 1 Cor. xvi. 2).
Illustrative helps (Matt. xiii. 34).
Music (Neh. xii. 46; 1 Chron. xv. 22).
Exercises (Col. iii. 16).
Spirituality (1 Cor. xiii. 1; 1 Cor. xiv. 15).

#### Hints to Teachers

Prepare yourself as well as your lesson.
A godly life is the best light for a lesson.
More important than knowledge, or the ability to impart it, is the power to stimulate in others a desire to know.

Give your scholars something out of each lesson that will help them to be a blessing at home and among their companions.

Use your Bible when teaching.    .

A lesson help in the hands of a teacher while in the class is, "like an iceberg between two lovers."

Speak up.  Be yourself.

Prepare conscientiously.

Know your Bible.

Always speak as for the last time.

Live what you preach.

"The aim of the teacher, who would find his way to the hearts and understandings of his hearers, will never be to keep down the parabolical element in his teaching, but rather to make as much and as frequent use of it as he can."—*Archbishop Trench.*

### Sunday School Teacher

#### John i. 40, 41.

1. The great object sought to be accomplished. Introduction to Jesus.  Interest in Jesus.  Instruction from Jesus.  Intimacy with Jesus.

2. Qualifications a teacher should possess.  Sincere and ardent piety.  An enlightened knowledge of Christ and His method of salvation.  Adaptation in the mode of instruction.  An exhibition of knowledge of Christ practically in life.

3. Effects resulting from attainment.  Christ will be glorified.  Church enlarged.  World will be benefited.  Your labours rewarded.

Note the importance of looking out for opportunity.

The value of union.

Therefore—Find, Tell, and Bring.

### Anecdote

"'Without a parable spake He not unto them.' For teaching, one illustration is worth a thousand abstractions.  Illustrations are windows of speech through which truth shines."—*E. P. Hood.*

### Talking to the Children

It is a gift, or an acquirement of no small importance, for teachers and preachers to be able to talk to children without becoming children, to be simple without being silly, adapting themselves to the condition of a child without being childish.

### Encouraging Thought for Parents and Teacher

The gospel involves no condition that a child cannot fulfil. It imposes no requirements that a child cannot meet. A child may trust its promises, realize its blessings, and anticipate its rewards.

The death of Jesus is the child's plea.

The grace of Jesus is the child's strength.

Pleasing Jesus is the child's easiest rule of right.

Going to be with Jesus is the child's best thought of heaven.

### Power in Work

In a factory containing 30,000 spindles, a wonderful sight. Motive power derived from two engines named Energy and Perseverance. Steam driven through Energy at great pressure and caused to pass through Perseverance. So in Christian work both these qualities should be found helping each other. Second controlling the first, the first invigorating the second. Peter and John both necessary. Work harmoniously. Joined in holy service. Power, God's Holy Spirit.

### "If ye seek Him, He will be found of you"

#### 2 Chron. xv. 2.

"To be a seeker," said Cromwell, "is to be one of the best next to a finder, for every faithful, humble seeker shall be a finder at last."

We may seek gold, and not get it ; health, and yet pine in sickness ; friends, and seek them in vain.

To seek God is to obtain His favour, to enjoy His smile, find mercy. He *will* be found. Is, then, God found of all? No. Why? Notice *If.* Finding comes after seeking. The finding depends on the seeking.

## SUNDAY SCHOOL ADDRESSES

### Anchors

#### Heb. vi. 19.

Their value.   Four required (Acts xxvii. 29).

Sight of them remind you of dangerous rocks.   In the storm of life need true one.   Some false ones, if trusted to *alone* : good feelings, good works, good resolutions, good friendships.

*v.* 19.   True hope.   Jesus the Pilot, Scriptures the compass, Hope the anchor, Faith the cable.

### Children's Voice of Praise

#### Ps. viii. 2.

Many men have been made to hold their tongues while children have borne witness to the glory of God of heaven.   He who delights in the songs of angels is pleased to honour Himself in the eyes of His enemies by the praises of little children.

Infant piety ; its potency, possibility, strength and influence.

Great results from small causes when the Lord ordains to work.

### Christ and the Children

#### Matt. xviii. 1–14.

To be good is to be great.   Real humility is true nobility (*v.* 4).

The value of an action is its being done in the name of Christ (*v.* 5).

Better suffer long than sin a little (*vv.* 7, 8).

To do good we must be good (*v.* 8).

Cruelty, not love, desires the punishment of sin (*v.* 9).

By their ruling we know the great ones of the earth. By their serving we know the great ones of heaven (*v.* 10).

The salvation of the least is worth the best efforts of the highest (*v.* 12).

God would save all, for Christ died for all (*v.* 14).

### Clean Hands

#### Ps. xxiv. 4.

Boys playing marbles to last minute, till meal-times or school-time.

Told not to meddle with ink. Disobey, and marks left for days.

David asks, "Who shall ascend the hill of the Lord?" God answers, "He that hath clean hands." Dishonest hands. Mother's sugar. Master's till.

Meddlesome and mischievous hands.

Cruel hands. Kindness to animals. Catching flies. Torture dumb animals. Flogging horses. Teasing dogs.

Murderous hands. Fighting spirit. Untamed temper leads to dreadful deeds.

Beautiful and useful hands. Kind acts. Helpful. Assisting mother. Threading grandma's needle. Acts of charity. A little help worth a deal of pity.

### Copper Precious as Gold

#### Ezra viii. 27.

Ask if gold or copper more valuable.

Two vessels of fine copper desirable as gold.

Common vessels. Little every-day acts. Common deeds, when well done, are as precious as greater ones.

Book of Golden Deeds, some wish to see their names in. But a better book, and larger one, in which we may be enrolled, called Common Deeds Well Done.

Play with younger brother when wanted. Self-denial.

Quality of copper : *fine*, polished, made to shine, like kettles.

Polish our deeds by gentleness, cheerfulness, unselfishness.

Let us do all common things well.

### Don'ts, A Few, for Boys and Girls

Serviceable to remember. If you don't need them, pass them on.

Don't say, "I won't." Prompt and cheerful obedience is like oil to the wheels.

Don't be always grumbling. Emptiest brains can grumble.

Don't think yourself wiser or cleverer than you really are.

Don't indulge in tall talk.

Don't wear two faces.

Don't look too much on the dark side of things.

### Five Members of the Body

*The Tongue.* If we belong to God, our tongues belong to Him, and they should be "kept" (Prov. xxi. 23); "wholesome" (Prov. xv. 4); "kind" (Prov. xxxi. 26); "soft" (Prov. xxv. 15); "bridled" (James i. 26).

*The Ears.* Four kinds in Bible. "Hearing" (Prov. xx. 12); "inclined" (Prov. iv. 20); "apt" (Prov. xxiiL 12); "attentive" (Neh. viii. 3).

*The Eyes.* Read about them. "Single" (Matt. vi. 22); "lifted" (Ps. xii. 1); "bountiful" (Prov. xxii. 9); "seeing" (Prov. xx. 12).

*The Feet.* To be worthy to stand before Him. "Shod" (Eph. vi. 15); "unmovable" (Ps. cxxi. 3); "beautiful" (Rom. x. 15).

*The Hands.* Four fingers. "Clean" (Ps. xxiv. 3, 4); "helpful" (Eccles. ix. 10); "diligent" (Prov. xii. 24); "wonderful" (Acts v. 12).

### Giants to Fight

Giant Sloth.

Giant Selfishness.

Giant Untruth.

Giant Hate.

Giant Pride.

### God as a Teacher

"*O God, Thou hast taught me from my youth.*"— Ps. lxxi. 17.

Every teacher and every teaching we have comes from God. Does the Bible teach us? The Bible is God's book. Do our friends teach us? Our friends are God's gift. He teaches wisely and well.

Many ways of teaching us. By example Jesus Christ taught us how to keep God's law. By His Spirit, makes things plain.

If He sends us, day by day, joys, it is to teach gratitude. If sorrow, then patience. If grief, to teach us our own sinfulness. If gladness, to teach us His love.

God is a patient teacher. We are slow to learn.

Many difficult lessons in the school of life, but Christ is our Schoolmaster.

### Goodness

#### Gal. v. 22.

Fruit of the Spirit is goodness. Some fruit is sour (say crab tree). Strawberry plant palatable. Children bear *fruit*. Goodness makes them willing to forgive wrongs. Would it be manly to resent wrong? Yes; but Godlike to forgive it.

Goodness teaches people to be considerate and generous.

Goodness prompts to be conscientious and enduring.

Goodness makes people heroic.

Therefore bear this fruit abundantly.

### Joseph as an Example

Loving to his father.
Forgiving to his brothers.
Honest to his master.
Helpful to his country.
True to his God.

### Keep this Gate Shut

Gates important things in country. Keep cattle from straying. Obey this notice, "Please shut this gate."

*Home Gate.* Have a bell if you like; don't leave the door ajar, else many things can enter. Englishman's house is his castle. Guard home as your own life. Keep pure and sacred.

*Sin Gate.* Cannot have too many padlocks and barricades between a man and evil. Temptation comes without invitation.

*Mouth Gate.* Keep it shut when required. A remedy for a cold is to keep the mouth shut. As we are careful what we eat, so be careful what we say. Think twice as much as you say. Beware of drink.

*Ear Gate.* Don't listen to evil, dirty talk. Nor backbiting nor slander. Open to God's voice, and obey His commands.

### Life, Weft of

Ps. cxxxviii. 8.

*Lessons from a Carpet Factory*—plain and rich velvet both made.

First room—wools of every shade, tangled heap.

Second room—women and children ; wools twisted and arranged in colours.

Designer painting upon paper patterns, and his great ideas worked out in factory. So in human life. Tangled mass seemingly, out of which a life may be made lovely by-and-by.

Every single thread in daily history worth thought and care.

Every detail in our lives taking its place in beautiful pattern if obeying the Designer's will.

Dark shades of trial and sorrow preparing for the bright ones.

Though patterns often are difficult to understand, yet planned by the wisdom of One who sees beginning and end.

Threads at back kept the whole, so if out of sight yet useful.

### Little Things

Importance of little things cannot be overrated.

Physical and tangible things around us.

Air we breathe, water we drink, etc.

A little worm in timber may eat away and sink the ship.

A little cold may lay the foundation of a continued illness.

"A little drop " will do no harm, 'tis said, but the sea of trouble is made up of drops.

Duty properly performed is simply well-doing in little things.

Great results from little causes spring.

Acorn parent of gigantic oak.

Life is made up, not of great deeds, duties, and sacrifices, but in little acts of daily duty.

### Making Sunshine

"*Let your light shine.*"—Matt. vi. 16.

A clever New Yorker tried to find out how to make sunshine. Failed, and apparatus burned. Beautiful idea. Possible for children and grown up.

Sunshine of the very best sort—cheerfulness, kindness, sympathy, and lovableness.

It is proper business of good people. "Ye are the light." Christ did it. Sad people He cheered. Sick people He cured. Blind people sight. He made sunshine for the widow of Nain, Jairus, and at Bethany. So He wants us to. But is it not hard to be always shining? Yes; but obtain light from the sun—Jesus. He is the Sun. Think of Him, read of Him, make Him your model.

So through life be always busy in the most beautiful of industries—making sunshine.

### Obedience

"*Doers of the Word, and not hearers only.*" — Jas. i. 22.

A mirror. To reveal ourselves. A girl looks to see her bonnet on straight, but forgets to put it right. A boy with dirty face sees the smut, but forgets to wash it clean. Strange; yet as hearers and not doers.

Four things which every one has who hears and heeds the Word of God,—

1. A quick ear. Hears at once, however softly spoken, as Samuel and Eli. Some hear and answer, but not obey.

2. Cautious tongue. Quick to hear, slow to speak. Bit in horse's mouth to guide. Children's tongues say untruths, unkind words. Little words quickly spoken cause great havoc.

3. A calm temper. Slow to anger. Hasty temper leads to dreadful results. Control early, or it will master you when older.

4. A pure heart. As hands and faces often want washing, so our hearts, if neglected, become fouled with sin. Cleansed through His word.

### Out of the Mouth Proceed, etc.

Matt. xii. 35.

1. W ords.
2. A ctions.
3. T houghts.
4. C ompanionships formed.
5. H eart's desires.

Therefore, to become a good soldier of Christ, *Watch.*

## Pins

### Exod. xxxv. 18.

Bible tells us of great things—Eternity, etc., God's great love, Heaven.

Also little things—Pins, Ants, etc.

A popular saying, "I don't care a pin."

Learn this : Smallest things are of use in God's service.

Tabernacle, Altar, and Ark, all held together with pins.

Children, though small, can do something and have a place in the world.

A boy in Boston went to a boot shop, and whilst waiting for his boots invited the errand boy to his school.  Did his part.  That errand boy was D. Moody, the evangelist.

Instance—Great ship, ironclad, yet go down and see the little apparatus that controls the helm.  Important, and unseen by many.

A good pin has a good point and head ; is straight, not crooked ; is bright, not rusty.

John Pounds, the cobbler, gathered his boys in his shop, talked to them.  So the outcome was, ragged schools were established.  Little things rightly used become mighty.

## Reading

### 1 Tim. i. 4.

Choose right books, good ones.

*For companionship.*  A good book is like a good friend—teaches us how to live.  "They soothe the grieved, stubborn they chastise, fools they admonish, and confirm the wise."

*For information.*  Read if you would know.

*For inspiration.*  Bible.  Bunyan.  In Acts 'tis recorded a bonfire of bad books.  The Bible.  Book of books.  Best of books.  Contains the maxims of heaven in human language.

Read it aloud, to old folks, to blind and unlettered.

Read it daily, as a guide, philosopher and friend.

Read it on your knees.  Seek Divine light.

The Word of God is His chosen instrumentality for the Church's progress and for the world's recovery. Then do all you can to circulate it.

### Real Hero, A

Dan. i.

Daniel probably an orphan, captive boy.

Battles he fought with pride, purposed in his heart, stood alone, taste.

Abstained from the king's tables and its dainties.

He spoke out boldly, made enemies.

Victory he gained. Clear conscience, undefiled body.

His faith strengthened and saved his three companions. These four eventually took foremost positions in state.

Remember, he who would fight for God and man must conquer self.

Do the right and look above.

### Roses

List of different varieties. Roses of fifty years, 1,500 kinds. Love is the Queen, the rose amongst Christian graces.

It is always one flower, like the Rose of Sharon, whence it sprang.

Innumerable varieties of development.

Every hue of heaven it bears, as by countless forms of beauty and shades of colour the great Infinite Love upon the eternal throne finds faint reflection.

### Samuel, The Child

1 Sam. iii. 1, 13.

The child of prayer, given to God and asked of God.

A dedicated child.
A converted child.
A ministering child.
A called child.
An obedient child.
An instructed child.
A listening child.
A rewarded child.

### Seeking God Early

"*I love them that love Me.*"—Prov. viii. 17.

I. GOD HAS A SPECIAL REGARD FOR CHILDREN.

Shown in His Providence and as author of parental affection, and in His Word and Commandments.

Christ the Son, once a child, and exemplified duties of childhood.

He encourages parents to bring children to Him.

II. It is an Important Matter to find God.

He is great ; He made and keeps all things, and is greater than all things.

III. How is He to be Found?

God needs to be sought. Where are we to seek? In Christ. In the Bible where He speaks. In prayer where He hears everywhere and always.

IV. The Promise is to those who Seek Him Early.

Early each day, in early life. The advantages. The promise : "Shall find Me." Early seed time ; early harvest. Delays are dangerous.

### Tempters

"*My son, if sinners entice thee,*" etc.—Prov. i. 10.

1. *A danger implied.* It is the nature of sin to be aggressive. No person was ever guilty of only one sin. On earth a huge propaganda of evil. Hence the danger to young and inexperienced.

2. *A method exposed*—"entice." The tempter proceeds indirectly and flatteringly. Enticements, an increase of knowledge, pleasure, love of liberty, nobody will ever know.

3. *Resistance enforced.* Consent thou not. Yes or no. Definite. No "yes" in your "no." Say it at the right time and right way. Remember this in moral actions, and necessity of choice in matters of conduct.

4. *The safeguard of holy memories.* My son. Open the book of memory at the page where a father's solicitude and a mother's love are recorded.

5. This may be viewed as *the utterance of God.* He unfolds to us His fatherhood in Christ and beseeches us to resist sin.

### Watchfulness

Mark xiii. 33.

Watch and pray.

Red lantern or flag, on rail or street, denotes danger. Lesson is to warn us from danger. Watch.

Watch against sin. If we knew our house would be visited by burglars we should prepare, take precautions, and watch. Sin lures. Like sheep on mountain side, tempted down from ledge to ledge, till unable to remount.

Watch for Christ. Queen Victoria first visited Edinburgh. Expected at 9 a.m., but arrived earlier —between 6 and 7. Officials too late. No welcome.

Wait for Him by doing loving acts, and giving help to others.

### Watch

W ords.
A ctions.
T houghts.
C ompanions.
H eart.

T emper.
H abits.
Y earnings.

L ips.
I nfluence.
F riendships.
E nemies.

### Youth of Jesus, Lessons to be Learned from the

#### Luke ii. 52.

True greatness is humble (*v.* 40).

Every child should be trained to Bible study (*v.* 42).

Never go a step without making sure Jesus is with you (*v.* 44).

It is a serious matter to lose communication with Christ (*v.* 45).

The places we frequent are an index of our character (*v.* 46).

Jesus is our Example as well as our Saviour (*v.* 51).

Silent hours are not lost hours (*v.* 51).

A holy life is pleasing to God, and attractive to good men (*v.* 52).

### Zacchæus

#### Luke xix. 1–10.

Verses 1–4. Sinner seeking Jesus.

Verse 5. Sinner seen by Jesus.

Verses 6–9.    Saved sinner serving Jesus.

J { Jesus
    Journeying to
    Jerusalem, halted at
    Jericho.

E { Entered house of Zacchæus, who
    Eagerly received Him, and
    Entertained Him joyfully.

S { Seeking Jesus, and
    Serving Jesus, Zacchæus was
    Satisfied by Jesus.

U { Uncharitable Jews
    Unable to
    Understand Jesus.    Why?

S { Son of man, who
    Sought and saved the
    Sons of Abraham,

Seeks and saves sinners still.

## TEMPERANCE TOPICS

Sir B. W. Richardson, the physician, says : " I have worked actively while indulging a moderate measure of alcohol daily, and also I have worked actively while abstaining.    So I can testify that the work that can be done during total abstinence is superior in every respect—in *amount, readiness of effort, quality*, and in respect to mental ease and happiness.

*Abstain* from all evil, even appearance, specially drink.

*Retain.*    By so doing we retain our love, our money, and happiness, and for others.

*Obtain.*    Such a life will lead us to obtain all blessings promised.

### Advice Gratis

| | |
|---|---|
| Drink less. | Breathe more. |
| Eat less. | Digest more. |
| Clothe less. | Bathe more. |
| Ride less. | Walk more. |
| Sit less. | Dig more. |
| Worry less. | Work more. |
| Waste less. | Give more. |
| Write less. | Read more. |
| Preach less. | Practise more. |

### Drink

Drink shops are called *inns*, a short word with a long list of meanings. Those who go to such places get *in*jury; become *in*decorous, *in*dolent, and *in*digent; get *in*famous and *in*firm. The inn makes some *in*solvent, *in*human, *in*sane, and all in some degree become *in*toxicated and *in*temperate.

### Drink

"As I look at the hospital wards, and see that seven out of every ten cases owe their disease to alcohol, I cannot but lament that the teaching about this question is not more direct, more decisive and home thrusting. Can I say any words stronger than these of the terrible effects of the use of alcohol? It is when I think of all this that I am disposed to give up my medical profession, to give up everything, to go forth on a crusade, preaching to men, Beware of this enemy of the race."—*Sir A. Clark.*

### Drink. Downward Steps

Descend.
    Deception.
        Despair.
            Disgrace.
                Disease.
                    Death.

### Example, Power of

Rev. C. Garrett tells of a lad, thirteen years old, who sat at the table with his father. Wine on table. "What will you take?" asked waiter of the boy. "I'll take what father takes." Father had the decanter in hand, about to pour out ;wine, but at these words loosed hold, and replied, "Waiter, I'll take water."

### Intemperance and the Bible

*Cause.* Gen. iii. 6; Num. vi. 3; Gen. ix. 20–25.
*Prohibition.* Prov. xxiii. 31, 32; Eph. v. 18; Isa. v. 22.
*Abstinence.* 1 Thess. v. 22; Rom. xiv. 21; Exod. xii. 19; 1 Cor. vi. 19, 20.

### Nation's Drink Bill

There are in the Old and New Testament together 3,566,480 letters. The money spent in strong drink for one year would enable us to place forty sovereigns on every one of those letters in the Bible.

### Pledge, Objections to the

Often stated, "I don't believe in pledges." Yet speaker was up to the ears in political, commercial, or social pledges. Enters into modern life largely. Every judge, M.P., magistrate, accepts a pledge and oath of allegiance to Queen. Ordinary affairs of life are crowded with binding pledges.

Pledge even in the Church. Minister at ordination; Sacrament a renewal of pledge. Hence, a safeguard and help to others.

### Temperance: as Plain as A B C

A  is for Ale, a poisonous drink ;
B  is for Beer, quite as bad, I think.
C  is for Cider, don't sip it, I pray ;
D  is a little Drop, throw it away !
E  stands for Earnings, which the wife wants at home,
F  is the Fool, with his money gone.
G  is the Gutter, where drunk he lies,
H  is the Horror, that glares from his eyes.
I  is the Illness, brought on by his folly ;
J  is that misused, mistaken word Jolly.
K  is his Kindness, long forgot ;
L  is the Lazy, lying sot.
M  is a Mocker : so Scripture calls wine.
N  stands for No ! say No ! next time.
O  is the Outcast, who thus shall return,
P  to Prosperity, as thousands learn.
Q  is for Quantity, take none at all.
R  for Religion, best safeguard of all.
S  is the Sober man, drunkard no longer :
T  is for Temperance, which makes him grow stronger.
U  stands for Use : soon changed to abuse.
V  is the Vine, which God gave us for use :
W  is Wine, the vine turned to abuse.
X  is for double X, as publicans know.
Y  stands for Yield ! for we'll soon lay them low !
Z  is for Zero, to which point they must go.

### Temperance, Need of

" The more I examine and travel over the length
and breadth of England, the more I see the absolute
and indispensable necessity of temperance organiza-
tions. I am satisfied that unless they existed we should
be immersed in such an ocean of immorality, violence
and sin as would make this country uninhabitable."—
*Lord Shaftesbury.*

The late Dean Hook tells this story—" When in
Leeds I had a man in my parish who earned eighteen
shillings a week ; out of this he gave his wife seven
shillings for housekeeping, the balance went in drink,
etc. I went to him and suggested this plan. ' Now
suppose you and I abstain for six months.' ' Will
you if I do ? ' asked the man. ' Yes, I promise.'
' From beer, wine and spirits ? ' he enquired.
' Yes.' ' And how shall I know you have kept
your promise ? ' ' Why, you ask my missis and I'll
ask yours ! ' It was agreed ; now he is a happy and
prosperous man of business, and I am Dean of
Chichester."

### Temperance

Aim of workers was to secure a sober country.

Portray a condition of universal contentment, health
and prosperity.

If Liverpool were sober for a week, the stores could
not equal the demand.

Boot shops would be sold out, hands would be
wanted everywhere.

Hope for future. A boy hearing of defeat, said :—
" Wait till we boys get the vote."

The children were the reserves.

Moderation was only an elastic band.

Drink is dear, deceitful, and destructive.

### Temperance Worker, Qualification of

Duty, Sense of.
Temper, Even.
Sympathy.
Common sense.
Punctuality.
Thoroughness.
Tact.
Benevolence of thought and action.
Humble-minded.

### Temperance Retrospect

#### Lev. xxv. 10.

Review waste that the drinking system has entailed upon our country during last fifty years.

Waste of food. As much food wasted in production of liquors as would feed three millions every year.

Waste of wealth. During fifty years of Queen's reign 4,500 millions spent in liquor.

Waste of life. 40,000 persons directly slain through intemperance, besides from hereditary taints.

Waste of social strength. Pauperism, crime, disease.

Waste of family welfare. Homes marred, disgraced. Buxton said thirty years ago that half a million families never knew family happiness through inroads and scourge of drink.

Waste of moral and spiritual power. Benevolence to rescue, remedy the plague. Hospitals, etc., Churches affected.

*Remedies.*—Rescue, prevention, education, legislation, and God's blessing.

### What Stops the Way

Rev. C. Garrett once, on his way to Exeter Hall to speak, found himself detained on a 'bus in Fleet Street, because of the block in traffic. Alighting and walking on found cabs, omnibuses, waggons, trucks, all at a standstill. The cause was the brewers' dray, delivering the barrels to a public-house. Typical of hindrances to all industrial, social, religious progress —the beer barrel.

## HELPFUL HINTS

### Business

The busiest are the happiest. "Employment so certainly produces cheerfulness," says Bishop Hall, "that I have known a man come home from a funeral quite in high spirits, because he had the management of it." "Work is the salt of life."

Do what you can and leave others to do what you cannot.

### Education

"The schoolmaster is abroad. I trust more to him, armed with his power, than I do to the soldier in full military array, for the upholding and extending the liberties of his country."—*Lord Brougham.*

### Falsehood

The first discourse ever preached had a lie for it text, and made converts of half of its hearers.

### Flattery

Like false money, it impoverishes those who receive it.

Godless science reads nature as Milton's daughter did Hebrew, rightly syllabling the sentences, but utterly ignorant of the meaning. Douglas Jerrold said, "I knew a man who could speak twenty-five languages, and he never said anything worth hearing in any of them." So, until the moral nature is open to truth, a man is blind to the real beauty and significance of the facts acquired.

### Grumbling

"Cart-wheels grumble and creak for want of grease, but often it is from want of work. You'll never give over creaking and grumbling till you do something. In heaven they rest not day or night. I know there will be no grumblers there, because they are all too busy."—*M. G. Pearse.*

### Health, Precious

It is a sum of money in the bank which will support you, economically spent. But you spend it foolishly and draw upon the principal. This diminishes the income, and you draw the oftener and the larger drafts until you become bankrupt. Over-

G

rating, overworking, every imprudence is a draft on life which health cashes and charges at a thousand per cent. interest. Every abuse of health hastens death.

### Inconsistency

An old quaint writer tells of men who talk by the pound and live by the ounce, who have heaven on their tongue's end and the world at their finger tips.

Life is a noise between two silences.

### Tact

Tact is the rudder of the ship, the little wheel behind the windmill, the tail of the kite, the ballast of the balloon, the feather on the arrow, and the rein on the restive steed.

### Proverbs—of Caution

The less men think the more they talk.

Think much, say little, write less.

Drop the jest when it is most amusing.

He who sows thorns should not go barefooted.

Nothing can come out of a sack but what is in it.

In diving to the bottom for pleasure we bring up more gravel than pearls.

### Proverbs

Life is like a pendulum swinging between a smile and a tear.

All clouds do not rain.

He who anticipates calamities suffers them twice over.

Better than allopathy and homœopathy is sympathy.

*Advice* is seldom welcome. Those who need it most like it least.

Idleness is hunger's mother, and of theft its full brother.

Better repair the gutter than the whole house.

Out of difficulties grow miracles.

Civility costs nothing, but it buys everything.

In the case of doubt lean to the side of mercy.

# INDEX OF TEXTS

## OLD TESTAMENT

Butler & Tanner, The Selwood Printing Works, Frome, and London.

### FOR TEACHERS

*Just Out. Narrow 8vo, 1s. 300 Outlines. Fifteenth Thousand.*

## Tool Basket for Preachers, Sunday-School Teachers, and Open-Air Workers.

Being a New Volume of Outlines of Addresses for Pulpit and Platform. A valuable Pocket Companion.

Rev. MARK GUY PEARSE says: "Admirable; the sort of thing that is simply invaluable to busy workers."

"The quality is very good and the number very great."—*Expository Times.*

---

**A Box of Nails** for Busy Christian Workers. 160 Bible Readings and Outline Addresses. By Rev. C. EDWARDS. Crown 8vo, 1s. 6d.

"Display real ingenuity and aptness. Strongly advise the investment."—*Primitive Methodist.*

**Talks to Young Folks.** By G. HOWARD JAMES. Crown 8vo, 2s. 6d.

"Simple, homely language; telling illustration."—*Christian Commonwealth.*

**Object Sermons in Outline.** By Rev. C. H. TYNDALL. Crown 8vo, 3s. 6d.

"The great kindergarten in the pulpit."—*Expository Times.*

**Revival Sermons in Outline.** Thoughts, Themes, and Plans, Original and Compiled. By C. H. PERREN. Crown 8vo, 3s. 6d. Just out.

**Seed Corn for the Sower.** A Book of Illustrations for the Pulpit and Platform. With Complete Indices to Subjects, Texts and Authors quoted. Cloth boards, 394 pp., 5s. Just ready.

A NEW VOLUME OF OBJECT SERMONS.

**What Shall I Tell the Children?** By Rev. GEO. O. REICHEL, M.A. Crown, 5s.

"Very useful to those who preach to children. Its merit is that it is fresh."—*British Weekly.*

---

H. R. ALLENSON, 30, Paternoster Row, E.C.

## Lectures on Preaching. By the Right Rev.
PHILLIPS BROOKS. Crown 8vo, 5s.

## The Influence of Jesus on the Moral,
Social, Emotional, and Intellectual Life of Man. By the
Right Rev. PHILLIPS BROOKS. Crown 8vo, 5s.

## The Life with God. Lenten Address by
PHILLIPS BROOKS. Post 8vo, neat artistic wrapper, 28 pp.,
6d. net, post free, 7d.

### By DR. BOYD CARPENTER.

## Thoughts on Prayer. By Right Rev. Lord
BISHOP OF RIPON. Fcap. 8vo, cloth, 1s. 6d. CONTENTS:
Necessity of Prayer—Times Adverse to Prayer—Heart-
work in Prayer—Reality of Answers to Prayer—Efficacy
of Prayer, etc.

"It deals with many important questions. Cannot but prove
helpful to all who may bestow any attention upon them. We
accord this volume a most hearty welcome."—*Rock.*

## Footprints of the Saviour. By Right Rev.
Lord BISHOP OF RIPON. Chapters on places visited by our
Lord: Bethlehem — Cana — Sychar — Nazareth — Caper-
naum—Gennesaret—Decapolis — Bethany—Gethsemane—
Calvary—Emmaus—Olivet. Crown 8vo, cloth, 2s. 6d.

### By DR. G. D. HERRON.

## A Plea for the Gospel. Cloth, 3s. 6d.

"Dr. Herron's work is so timely, so original, and so vigorous,
that it receives the heartiest welcome."—*Golden Rule.*

## The Christian State. A Political Vision of
Christ. By Rev. G. D. HERRON, D.D. Fcap. 8vo, cloth,
3s. 6d.

## The New Redemption. A Call to the Church.
By Rev. G. D. HERRON, D.D. Fcap. 8vo, cloth, 3s. 6d.
Sixth Thousand.

"A book to be read and pondered."—*American Independent.*

## Sunday Mornings at Norwood. By Rev. S.
A. TIPPLE. With Four Additional Sermons and Prayers.
Second Edition. Crown 8vo, cloth, 6s.

## The Spirit of Truth. Sermons by JOSEPH
HALSEY, Author of "The Beauty of the Lord." Crown
8vo, 5s. Very fresh sermons.

## The Spirit of the Age. By D. J. BURRELL,
D.D. 5s.

## Christ at the Door of the Heart, and other
Sermons. By Rev. MORGAN DIX, D.D. Crown 8vo,
cloth, 366 pp. 3s. 6d. CONTENTS: Advent—Close of the
Year—Epiphany (3)—Septuagesima—Lent (3)—Easter (3)
—Passion Sunday—Idle Fears, etc.

---

H. R. ALLENSON, 30, Paternoster Row, E.C.

**A Young Congo Missionary:** Memorials of Sidney Roberts Webb, M.D. By William Brock. Handsome cloth, crown 8vo. Just out. 2s. 6d.

**Roberts of Tientsin ;** or, For Christ and China. By Mrs. Bryson. With Portrait and Preface by Rev. F. B. Meyer, B.A. Large crown 8vo. 3s. 6d. Second Edition.

"A better tonic for doubting minds than the brightest discussion of difficulties."—*Sunday School Times.*

**Joseph Sidney Hill** (First Bishop in W. E. Africa). By R. E. Faulkner. Three Portraits. Second Edition. Large crown 8vo, 3s. 6d.

"It is just the book to give away, particularly to young men and boys."—*C. M. Gleaner.*

**The Dominion of Christ.** By Rev. William Pierce. Handsome cloth, large crown 8vo, 3s. 6d. Special Edition, stout paper, 1s. net, for distribution.

Contents : Patriotism and Missions—The Vocation of the Missionary—Women as Missionaries—Place of Education as a Missionary Agency—Churches and Work of Foreign Missions—Physician and Evangelist, etc., etc.

**Heroic Endeavour.** A Word of Hope to Young Men. By Rev. W. Elsworth Lawson. Narrow 8vo. Artistically printed and bound, 1s.

"Of very considerable merit. It is able and strong, and full of suggestion."—*Young Man.*

**Christian Chivalry.** By Rev. Thomas Phillips, B.A. An Address to Young Men in the Cause of the Kingdom. An artistic booklet. Narrow 8vo, 6d.

An eloquent and stirring appeal to young men to follow Christ. Burns with missionary zeal. Based on St. Paul's words, "I can do all things through Christ which strengtheneth me."

**From our Dead Selves to Higher Things.** By F. T. Gant, F.R.C.S. Crown 8vo, 2s. 6d. A capital book for young men and women.

**Helen Murdoch; or, "Treasures of Darkness."** By Alice Jane Muirhead. Handsome crown 8vo, 256 pp., 2s. 6d.

"A story of trials bravely met ; is altogether wholesome and profitable, as well as full of absorbing interest."—*Christian.*

**Martyrs of Hell's Highway.** By Rev. H. Elwyn Thomas. A novel with a purpose. Preface and Appendix by Mrs. Josephine Butler. Written with passionate earnestness. Crown 8vo, cloth, 3s. 6d.

**In the Land of the Harp and Feather.** A Series of Welsh Village Idylls. By Alfred Thomas. Handsome crown 8vo, art cloth, gilt top, 6s.

**Tyne Folk: Masks, Faces, and Shadows.** By Dr. Joseph Parker, Minister of the City Temple, London. Crown 8vo, 3s. 6d. A graphic and pathetic narrative of peasant life in Northumberland.

H. R. ALLENSON, 30, Paternoster Row, E.C.